ARCADE RAT

NICHOLAS MORINE

ARCADE RAT

NICHOLAS MORINE

Published in Canada by Engen Books, St. John's, NL.

Library and Archives Canada Cataloguing in Publication

Morine, Nicholas, author
     Arcade rat / Nick Morine.

ISBN 978-1-926903-83-5 (softcover)

     I. Title.

PS8626.O74954A89 2018   C813'.6   C2018-903716-4

Distributed by:
Engen Books
www.engenbooks.com
submissions@engenbooks.com

First mass market paperback printing: August 2018

Cover Image: Shutterstock

This novel is dedicated to the memory of Sheriff Garba
of Biu, Nigeria.

River of Regret
I do not suffer myself regrets —
For no voyage is as fruitless as a voyage
On the River of Regret.
And yet there comes a time
When a man's body wings around in the sky of sadness
When his feet perch on the twigs of nostalgia.
-- Sheriff Garba, "River of Regret"

This story also goes out to all the guys out there with quarters
on the top of the cabinet, waiting their turn to be king.

CHAPTER 01
HAS BEEN

The sky was black, the stars blocked by dead skyscrapers. Rainwater slid down the knife-edged angles of the architecture like blood from a fresh wound. The streets were empty, broken beer bottles and countless expired coupons littering the roadway like confetti from an ancient war parade.

The booths, like a drug, called to him. Kaine couldn't bring himself to look at their smooth, contoured shells, the bright pastel glow emanating from them. With nothing but the staccato beat of the downpour to accompany his long walk home, the tin ringing of the gaming booths called out to his soul -- a siren song.

Play me.

Touch me.

Show them.

Show yourself.

His hands jerked involuntarily. He stuffed them into his pockets, feeling the thin fabric give way, touching the holes and probing them. He'd sew them up after taking a few more shots when he got back to the trailer. His leg hurt with every step he took, a deep ache that sharpened up as the weight of his frame came down on it. He limped along in the near pitch black night, trying to fend off the voices of his vices.

The headset around his neck vibrated, rattling a few loose pieces of metal inside the housing. Probably the wife wondering where the fuck he was at such an hour, berating him on his drunkenness, or accussing him of plowing yet another midnight mistress. Two or three hours late for that, at least. Kaine reached a small, calloused hand up to his neck to touch the sleep button.

No more distractions.

He stood next to a flower shop, the cheap tablet in the window advertising a sale long over. Hard business to be in when VR environments allowed lovers to exchange bouquets in the blink of an eye for free amidst fully sculpted gardens for the prize of a cheap pizza. Still some romantics in the world keeping the place alive, Kaine imagined, giving a silent salute to the smudged storefront before continuing down the beaten concrete. The tablet display dissolved from the overdue special to a stock photograph as he turned away.

Best booth in the city was a few blocks down. Cleaned yesterday, a corpse pulled from the small container in a clean black bodybag less than twenty-four hours prior. Kaine had been on the way to the unemployment office to collect his subsidy when he saw the crew pulling the remains from the enclosure.

Tightest joystick, the springs providing perfect resistance. The buttons recently greased, providing smooth push and pull-back. The gloves were tight, fresh leather and wiring. No faulty connections, no sticky residue from spilled liquor, or vomit. All of these could be lethal, but the addicts and the drunks that frequented the booths could not discern the difference. Cigarette burns aplenty, but the cosmetics of the interior didn't concern him.

Once the helm was worn, the world faded away. As it should. As it would.

The cans around his neck vibrated again, irritating him. With an annoyed snort, he slipped them onto his ears and turned down the synthwave that had been playing in the background.

"Yeah?" he muttered. The built in mic would pick up anything he said and relay it to the caller.

"You coming home or what?" a waspish tone slunk into his eardrums. It was Julia, as he'd suspected.

"Why? You can't take care of the kids yourself? I've got shit to do," Kaine said.

There was a dread silence on the other end, then the blip signaling a disconnection. He'd pay for that remark when he finally did arrive back at the trailer park, of this he was certain. A dead bedroom was the continuing campaign. It didn't intimidate him in the least; he was used to the sensation of crawling over broken glass that was his ill-considered marriage.

The synthwave returned and with it a sense of purpose. He was going to play tonight. Haunting keyboards and robotic percussion beat out a heavy track that impelled him forward. The few unbroken streetlights dotted the path in front of him, circles of trash pushed together at their base. Crumpled beer cans, bleached cigarette butts, and cheap chip foil mingled together in a stew of the underclass. The only souls that dared the streets at this hour, far from the safety of the gated communities and guarded apartment complexes the rest of society called home. If Kaine met a fellow traveller down this black boulevard, he could be sure they were as bitter as he was.

Kaine heard a whispering above his head, cutting through the mix. He tilted his neck upward and caught a glimpse of a surveillance drone out on patrol. Foot police were a figment of the past in UBI blocks, reserved for more appropriate settings or emergencies only. Bright LED lights spelled out the brand name of his favourite beer, eliciting a cheap smile from Kaine as the slight machine slipped away from him, taking a high and tight turn around the edge of a nearby skyscraper.

At least the drone had good taste. More likely it was a calculated demographic advertisement. Kaine knew that the drone had likely spied him, associated him with his profile via facial recognition, and then displayed the advertisement to him personally as an incitement to buy. No need for that -- mere wasted electricity -- as Kaine planned to buy another case before he sat in the booth.

The store and the booth sat adjacent, on the periphery of Kaine's vision as he ambled up the street to the pulsing beat. A bright star in an otherwise barren galaxy, the 24/7 was one of a thousand micromarts wedged into corner shops and down janky alleyways strewn about the city. Never more than a mile away, and open every hour of every day of the year, the 24/7 was where most poor people bought the fixtures of life. A paper-thin awning sprawled out from the giant windows facing an empty street, shot through with light emitting diodes that unctuated like the ocean, showing deep discounts on bananas and strong coffee -- projected in all colours of the rainbow.

Kaine stepped up to the doors and they slid apart, whining, grating with the effort.

"Doors could use a little grease," Kaine barked to the vaguely-human automaton across the counter.

"Yes sir. Noted," came the crisp reply in a thin tenor. The servos that supported the head slash monitor whirred as the robot nodded its non-understanding.

Kaine growled out an unintelligible reply, starting to feel a headache coming on -- the first sign of a brutal hangover. He spied the thin glass of the beer cooler in its familiar corner, flanked by retro fluorescent bulbs that reminded him of his childhood. An oasis of organization in a sea of clutter, the beer cooler displayed the cheapest brands known to the public, a variety of macrobrews that went down easy. The craft beer he'd used to swill during his younger years was a distant memory, something seen in advertisements rather than stores, and fully beyond the reach of his pocketbook. Plus, as he'd recalled, he'd never found it tasted better in any case.

The aisles of the 24/7 were towering above him, reaching nearly twelve feet to the ceiling. Items on the top shelp sported a thick coating of dust, but were still available at the standard retail price. Each facing of tins and pre-packaged food was accompanied by a thin panel displaying the cost in lime green relief. From the counter, the droid could alter any price at will, or dispatch a small birdlike surrogate to snatch the item from the shelf. Nonetheless, slow-moving SKUs were sent to the highest levels, beyond reach and beyond eye level, relegated to commercial ob-

scurity and effective nonexistence. Sometimes Kaine for-
got that vienna sausages and canned asparagus existed
-- just like every other customer of the micromart.

Boxes of prepacked rice, noodles, soups, gravies, and
meat flanked him as he limped down the towering aisle
to the beer cooler. The labels were always bright primary
colours, emblazoned with enormous yet simplistic brand
logos. Subtlety was a lost art in 21st century advertising,
although competition was just as much of an illusion
-- there were only a handful of corps on Earth and they
spawned sub-brands which pretended to compete for the
satisfaction of a beholden clientele. In reality, the differ-
ences were marginal at best. The recipes were the same
with minute differentiation, in infinite combination, offering a mirage of choice.

Kaine just bought whatever was cheapest that day.
Except for the beer, which had to be Red Baron. As he
told many of his drinking buddies -- his favourite beer
was free, his second favourite was Baron. Not that he had
many drinking buddies left. Most had died from liver or
kidney failure or cancer or depression or near anything
else father time could think to inflict on a poor soul.

He ran a hand over his small, slack belly, scratching
an itch that was never satisfied. The inconstant fluores-
cents lit the cooler as if it were a gift from the heavens.
The pure white luminescence was reflected perfectly by
his aviators, which Kaine never removed except to sleep.
The ocular implants the state had paid for when he was
still on the payroll would compensate for the low-light
conditions in any case -- the result was a darker, yet still
sharp vision of a matching world.

Red Baron filled a quarter of the slim cooler, an entire two shelves to itself. The sneering yet savage machismo of Manfred von Richtofen, leaning casually in full pilot's attire against his iron-crossed Fokker, was splashed like a wax stamp across the side of the crimson cardboard case. Kaine opened the glass pane and pulled a case free with a grunt of effort. Not as strong as he had been when he still walked a beat.

Kaine sat the beer down on the counter glass, the beer bottles clinking together as he did so. A small ten-inch tablet was wedged into the corner of the backstock area, above a small window. The front-facing camera simultaneously recorded the goings-on of the shop while projecting a live feed of the store back to the customer, a silent and polite warning against criminal intent.

"Will that be everything, Detective Kaine?" the AI chimed.

"Not a detective anymore. Title's a formality for old farts. Told you this a dozen times already you heap of junk," Kaine rasped laconically.

"Of course, Mr. Kaine. Upon your request, I have temporarily suspended your formal title in favour of your stated preference."

"Thanks."

"Will that be everything, Mr. Kaine?"

"Yeah. I mean..."

"Of course we do have several items on special. Packets of All-American Ramen Bowls are currently on sale for a dollar each. Dehydrated assorted fruit pieces are..."

"I don't eat fruit. Give me a bowl of the damned ramen. Beef. Microwave it for me."

The robot shrugged in the rough approximation of assent, and spun about on its torso to pull a plain white bowl from beneath the counter.

"Flash frozen vegetables included for merely an extra dollar?"

"Do it. Then the wife can't bitch about how I never eat anything green. Get it on the receipt."

"As you wish, Mr. Kaine. A moment, please."

As the micromart machine set to preparing the instant ramen dish, pouring hot water from the sink purifier into the bowl and shaking a packet of sickly looking peas, Kaine tore open the top of the cardboard box and slid his hand inside. Snatching a bottle free, ice cold in his palm, he twisted the cap off in one smooth motion and dumped it into the small white trashcan next to the counter.

"Before you say anything, I'm squaring up now. The customer is always right." Kaine leaned his wrist against the near-field communications panel and tapped his assent to pay. The robot, which had turned around in protest to sampling the merchandise before it had been processed, merely return to its stewardship of the pot noodles. A smart-looking sign proclaiming THE CUSTOMER IS AL-WAYS RIGHT hung, spotless, beside the camera tablet. It even held the large, bold 24/7 logo in the top right corner, adding a degree of officiality that seemed hard to argue with.

The beer was so cold that it bordered on being frozen, the frosted glass clinging to the soft flesh of his fingers as he tilted it to his lips. A faint bitterness, the cloying mainstay of the hops, rushed about his mouth before being swallowed. He took another long haul, gulping the lager down with intent. Thirty seconds remained on the microwave, and by now the robot, with nothing left to do, observed Kaine with dispassionate eyes. The advanced display that it called a face was moulded into an oval shape, fringed with stylized rubber. It displayed a primitive face while speaking, deals of the day at times, and absolute blackness to conserve power when the micromart was empty.

The beer was gone by the time the microwave beeped a trio of times and shut off.

"Your order, sir," The robot said, bowing slightly as it passed the steaming bowl over to Kaine. "…there is a table and chairs outside if you prefer --"

"Don't prefer. Prefer to eat it right goddamn here, as usual," Kaine cut the bot off, cracking another brew and waiting for the steam to stop rising from the boiled bouillon.

"As you wish, Mr. Kaine," the robot nodded exactly as it had before, to the micrometer. If the internal circuitry replacing synapses could convey irritation, they would have. But they did not, and the bot did not, either.

A long but comfortable silence followed, only the hum of electricity and the intermittent sound of a swallowed beer and ahhs of satisfaction punctuated the stillness. Kaine closed his eyes, one hand warm on the side of the bowl, the other lifting the thin mouth of the Baron to his mouth. Then, it too was empty, and he placed it along with the other dead soldier into its place in the case, hefting a third free. His headache was an afterthought, clinging to the back of his brain, about to be washed away in a tide of alcohol and savoury salt.

"You see the body they pulled from the other suicide

booth?" Kaine mumbled, slurping the warm broth and trying to herd the noodles with a plastic fork in his free hand. He pressed them against the side of the bowl while he let the spicy liquid splash over his tongue. It mixed with the cold beer in his gut and produced a pleasurable warmth that ran the length of his spine. The beef flavour was strong and dark and wholesome. A few stray peas escaped the guard of the plastic tines and found their way free.

"I thought you weren't a detective any longer, Mr. Kaine," the robot replied flatly. Kaine arched an eyebrow at the neutral expression displayed on the automaton's facial screen.

"And I thought micromart AIs weren't supposed to act like smartasses, not having the processing power for a sense of humour. But here we are."

Ignoring the repartee, the bot responded to the initial query.

"Yes, I saw the police cordon off the area, and the body being removed. Not directly, mind you, as the scene is precisely 1.4 miles from this location, but I observed via the surveillance camera network during my regular monitoring. As you know, I am constantly scanning all security footage available to me within a five mile radius of this location, in tandem with my 24/7 associates doing the same for their own locations."

"Too much information, C-3PO. I already know all that, besides," Kaine barked, chuckling to himself into his soup bowl. When it appeared his joke wasn't about to get a rise out of his conversation partner, his grin soured. He hammered the rest of his third beer after draining the bowl of broth, then returned to his line of questioning.

"So, how many cops? Did they mention what game he was playing? The stakes?"

"Five officers were present. One sergeant, one detective sergeant, three constables. He was apparently dead last in a game of Retro. Your specialty. Would you like to see the footage?"

"Yeah. Throw it on-screen," Kain said.

The bot's face dissolved into a vertical video in 4K resolution.

The camera was mounted on a streetlamp, overlooking a stretch of road that Kaine instantly recognized as on Montaigne Street, a regular feature on his walk back to the trailer court. A rusted and bowed chainlink fence served as the backdrop, home-made decals wrapped around the galvanized metal advertising local punk bands and unpopular politicians. The streetway itself was dimly lit and only the reflective police tape was visible. The suicide booth was front and center, the camera positioned perfectly, allowing full view of the entrance hatch.

In time lapse, skipping frames and looking choppy, the officers arrived on scene. As soon as they did, the video feed increased its depth of field and boosted frames until it was indistinguishable from watching it live. The blue and red flashers strobed against the smooth skin of the suicide booth and splashed against the wet concrete of the sidewalk and street. Hushed voices decided amongst themselves who would be first to open the hatch and observe the grisly interior. Finally, the Sergeant delegated, and a squat but muscular looking constable ambled forth and hauled on the manual release level, popping the rectangular portal open.

A bundle of rotten clothes and pale flesh tumbled forth, head cracking against the pavement with a soft sound. The police officers all took a step back; the constable whom had pulled the lever shrunk away from the corpse reflexively. The detective, a tall and lean plain-clothes officer, put down his vape pen and blew a huge plume of water vapour and nicotine. He knelt beside the dead man and reached a hand out to touch his face and neck, first checking the pulse and then the temperature of the skin.

"Gone. Tonight's loser. Bag him," he said, signalling with the two fingers cradling the pen for the constables to get to work. The detective stood in one smooth motion and walked away from the scene and out of camera view, long leather coat flapping at the back of his knees.

In moments, the three constables had managed to awkwardly stuff the body into a piano black bag.

"That's it boys. Call in the cremation team and let's get the hell out of here," the Sergeant barked. The men gave tired salutes. The short man tapped his fingers to his ear and made the call. In a matter of seconds, he gave the hand signal.

"Clean-up is en route Sarge. We done here?"

"Yeah," the gruff, older looking officer replied. Then the four remaining policemen scattered to the four winds and the video returned to time lapse, showing the cremation team arriving on-site, hefting the body bag, tossing it onto a truck bearing the state logo, and then disappearing into the night.

The robot face returned as the surveillance feed fell

away.

"Anything interesting, Mr. Kaine?"

"Just more of the same stupidity. Thanks," Kaine said, gripping the handholds on his box of beer and leaving the depleted bowl on the countertop as he turned toward the exit of the micromart. "And don't forget about those goddamned doors."

"Noted sir," came the steely speaker-voice to his back as the doors whined with his exit.

He was alone. He could hear the voice again. The pain in his leg was gone, dulled by the alcohol swimming through his veins.

Play me.

Touch me.

Show them.

Show them.

The giant crystalline structures that loomed above him, slick with rain, closed in upon him like mountains. He felt small beneath their constant shadow, which the sun could barely break. The downpour had intensified, now thick droplets of water slapped him in the face, beating against his shades, streaming into his beard.

Kaine cracked another beer and put his hand against the red button that opened the door to the suicide booth. The sour taste of the beer mingled with the fresh cold rainwater on his tongue as hea leaned against the side of the squat structure.

Just enough time for one last game. He brought the soggy cardboard case with him and slammed the hatch, severing contact with the world outside.

CHAPTER 02
THE WORLD THAT WAS

The sky was cerulean, the sun a hot and open eye graced by gossamer threads of cloud cover. The boys were loaded up in Bill's old teal Neon, fat with roadside cheeseburgers and store-brand cola. The small engine thrummed, vibrating the frame of the car as they drifted along winding country roads, following the promise of hidden gems in the form of dirty cartridges, bleached manuals, and crusty plastic.

"This flea market really s'posed to be fifty miles long?" Zack wondered aloud. He fidgeted with the belt buckle pinching at his dragon shirt. "Feels like we're stopping constantly!"

"Odometer don't lie. We're at thirty already," Bill replied. He was focused on the drive, paying scant attention to the bullshit his buddies were throwing around.

The trunk of the sedan was filled to bursting with treasures. A small shoebox of early generation transforming robots, a few turtles and rubber wrestlers mixed in. A stack of old wargames, all hexes and tokens and reams of rulebooks. Ricky Kaine's personal quest -- a collection of vintage video games, black shells bearing science fiction labels, clacking around against each other as the suspension road over the beaten and broken asphalt of the back roads. One last item -- a giant plush goblin, blue with a white cap and a dopey grin. The boys hadn't decided who was taking that home yet.

"You guys think those were Sunshine burgers? Kinda got that savoury breadcrumb taste to 'em," Josh asked from the back seat. He was wearing a bandana and cheap sunglasses they'd bought at the dollar store five miles back. It was beginning to dampen with sweat despite the air conditioning struggling to beat the heat.

"Not sure but for a buck, who cares? They were damn good. That old man knows how to grill!" Ricky belched at the last, rubbing his stomach. They all laughed over a Def Leppard track.

"Any cheeseburger is a damn good cheeseburger. I think I see our next stop. Pull over!"

Bill whipped the wheel hand over hand, pumping the brakes. Gravel slid beneath the tires and a plume of cinnamon dust spouted out behind the neon, then overtook them, carried with the wind. Four boys exited the beaten ride, slamming the doors.

They found themselves in a church parking lot. An elderly lady, stooped over, hands moving with deliberation, worked a small barbeque. Heat rose from the hood, blurring the treeline behind her. Birdsong chimed alongside the treble harmony of Joe Elliott and the boys coming from the open windows of the Dodge.

Long, lean tables were covered by mismatched tablecloths, the edges fluttering in the slight breeze. Some bore tassels, some missing plastic crystals. The church stood modestly as a backdrop, brickwork with modest mauve trim. The sign of the cross was painted white on cracked wood. A tall woman, thick amber glasses astride a pert nose, turned from a parting customer to greet them.

"Hello boys! Wonderful afternoon!"

Zack feigned interest in the porcelain angels and collectible spoons in dusty plastic boxes as he went to work.

"Absolutely, miss. Not often we make it out this far from home but doing the yard sale for the day!" He said. His smile was easy and guileless. Paired up with his thin polyester button-up emblazoned with a garish fantasy dragon and aviators, Zack cut a memorable figure. He was the fast talker, though they were all negotiators.

As Zack and the woman continued their conversation, the rest of them set to scavenge. Battered cardboard boxes rested in irregular rows beneath the sagging plywood tabletops. Bill and Josh knelt with whispered curses to dig through the treasures held within while Ricky strolled the length of the layout, quickly sorting out categories he knew he -- or the others -- would be familiar with.

Collectibles. Action figures. Cereal boxes. Pulp novels, long out of print, sunbleached. Game systems. Consoles. Old computers. Comic books. Old computer games, vibrant box art stolen from the imagination of Frazetta and Bakshi and other countless, nameless artists. An impure industry, nascent, boldly creative and yet amateur. The reason the boys were so hungry for a nostalgia that had not yet begun was because, curious and intelligent, they sensed the birth of a new cultural era. They were simply to archive and perhaps profit from the low-class, low-art prophecy.

Old folks used to call it a hunch. So on that hunch, and in good spirits all, Zach, Bill, Ricky, and Josh dug deep. Voices bantered back and forth over a given price. Lower, then lower. The older ladies were from a generation of horse traders, but the young gentlemen were ruthless and knowledgable. The latter won out, though all sides benefited and were in the highest spirits.

A couple deals later and cash exchanged and hotdogs downed, the boys piled back into the teal beater. The pair of ladies waved goodbye, grinning, corners of their eyes crinkled with age and the sun.

"Admit it, Zack. You had the hots for that one," Bill said, pointing subtly at the woman tending the barbeque. The engine rolled over then purred to life as he turned the key in the ignition.

Zack whistled dismissively as the rest of the boys laughed.

"What can I say bud? I like my ladies with a bit of experience, you know?" Zack said after a beat. The laughter returned and redoubled. Bill cracked, lips parting in a smile.

"Like you know a damned thing about ladies, Zack!" Ricky chimed in, flipping though a small stack of water-damaged comics he'd picked up for a dollar. Worthless on the secondary market, but worth a dollar for the stories -- Ricky reasoned with himself. "You check yourself out in a mirror lately? Girls not exactly loving the Dungeons and Dragons look."

This boyish cruelty was a special double edged sword, part cut, part compliment. It was a weapon only wielded when one was a true friend, warriors but brothers in life. In an age of postmodern savagery, the verbal was the remnant of the physical. That's not to say that fists never flew and that words were all that was ever exchanged. But talk was cheaper and cost less.

"Hey man, at least I can afford a shirt with a collar!" Zack shot back, turning about in the front seat to leer at Ricky. Zack flamboyantly positioned his aviators in the bridge of a clearly sunburned nose. Ricky looked down at his slightly stained muscle shirt.

Ricky grabbed the smaller boy by the lapels of this thin polyester shirt, fingers pulling at the buttons.

"Maybe I'll just borrow yours then, Frodo," Ricky rasped. Then he let go. Zach sprang back in his seat, back banging into the dash.

"Careful, moron! Your fat ass is going to set off the airbags!" Bill called out, slapping at Zach with his free hand.

Zach sat down and threw the finger at Bill. He straightened the collar of his shirt in ostentatious fashion.

The car and its passengers wound through the province, meandering through the heart of their homeland. Tall trees with regal crowns of pine and spruce stood proud alongside maples and oak. Modest houses, many mobile homes, rolled by on either side. Oftentimes the grass was freshly cut, with children playing in small, colourful pools.

Every so often there would emerge a body of water. Flat, with the smallest of waves, deep blue mixed with mud near the periphery. The soil was rich here, clay on the coast and fertile inland. Every one of them had grown up within a stone's throw of a farm, or a garden, or an array of fields, each larger than a millionare's estate. Truth was easy here and was delivered in even tones, from the tongue or by the whisper of the wind through the cornhusks. It was the song of swamp frogs calling for a midnight mate. It was the politeness and pleasantries exchanged by the same stalwart ma and pop behind the convenience store counter just down the lane.

It was an anchor. It was home. It was a place to go when the sun began to hang low.

It was a place that resisted the passage of the years and seemed immortal in its own way.

The young men reclined in their seats, talking shit. Blades of grass and loose gravel bowed at their passage.

They were so small under a dusken, cloudless sky.

CHAPTER 03
THE KING OF ARCADES

When Ricky Kaine walked into the arcade, time stood still. The bright blinking lights mellowed and the metallic chugging of pinball machines were background noise to his procession. Kids lined up behind the battered cabinets snatched their quarters from between the buttons and ran to mob their king. It was a small town and everybody knew one another, the young ones most of all. Rat moustached teens lowered their eyes as he passed, deferential despite the rebellious t-shirts and the headphones about their neck blaring hair metal. The darkness punctuated by effervescent neon was his throne-room, a place where he held court.

A potbellied man in his forties approached, wearing a stained referees shirt and too-tight khakis.

"Hey there, Ricky. Need change?" A fanny pack wrapped about his girth jingled with coin.

"Yeah, ten," Ricky replied from behind his shades, which he never removed until it was time to play. The arcade manager saw himself take the crumpled bill in the mirrored lenses. He was shorter than the teenager by a head, and was a closeted fan himself. Ricky was cool beyond measure. Even the kids from the city knew better than to take him on in nearly any game on the premises. Beyond the lean teenager's shoulder, the manager could see a slow stream of traffic heading down the dull brown promenade that was the small mall's thoroughfare, mostly women toting purses and pointing children, their fingers raised and eyes wide at the electronic paradise they were denied -- for now.

Soon enough Ricky found himself with a fistful of quarters and a burning desire to perform. His fans surrounded him, slackjawed, waiting to see which game he'd come to dominate today. Street Fighter II was the latest and greatest, but the computer challenger wasn't any real competition and there was nobody within a hundred miles who could offer even token resistance to Ricky's onslaught of fists, feet, and projectiles. Mortal Kombat was much the same, but less technical, relying on blood and gore and a deep-voiced narrator to put the iron in the spine. The racing simulators and dogfighters had their allure, and more than once Ricky had wowed the audience by nimbly navigating each level of Afterburner, still wearing his trademark aviators, riding the pneumatic thrust as if born to fly.

Ricky preferred the classics, the games which got harder and faster until you died. Game Over was a certainty, the beauty of the play was to see how long one could last against an increasingly unfair program. Sometimes, after hours of hand cramps and painful battle against the program, Ricky could force the game to glitch out and shut down. This, to him, was the only satisfactory victory. Man over machine. Man over a machine programmed by a much older, wiser, and smarter man to be completely impervious to defeat. Cheating the system and winning put a smile on the laconic teen's face.

Pac-Man, Donkey Kong -- Ricky had conquered them all in turn. Death after death produced new ways, new avenues, new paths of resistance that allowed him to gain a further foothold -- and eventually won. He would often lean against the heavily postered walls of the arcade, drinking from a pocket flask he'd spirited from his mother's trailer, watching other poor players make mistakes on the same machine he was at war against. Their mistakes became his lessons, their quarters saving the metal in his pocket from going to waste. He would spend entire evenings nestled between two machines, the heat from the cathode ray tubes and hot wiring radiating from the wood of the cabinets, warming him in tandem with the liquor. A few of the older teens might spy him at his post and trade him loose cigarettes for his hints and tips. The buzz was permanent and never faded until he began his walk home at the end of the night, his initials carved into pixelated glory.

A new game had come to Starr-cade, so named after the owner, Mr. Starr. Ricky had met him a few times and had liked him well enough. A giant of a man that towered tall over him, always smelling of strong cologne and an afterthought of smoke, Mr. Starr had offered Ricky a part-time job when he turned sixteen next year. Ricky was wise enough for his age to entertain the offer, and to flatter Mr. Starr in return. Ricky and Mr. Starr both knew he was good for business, and their amicability was based not over any shared love of video games, but a shrewd pragmatism that benefited them both. More money for Mr. Starr, more money and more game time for Ricky. Time to play games like the latest threat from Japan -- Bakunawa.

Roped off by crude chain hanging between steel poles set to either side, and with a thick carpet rolling up to the foot of the machine, Bakunawa taunted him. Bakunawa. Nobody knew what it meant but it sounded cooler than hell. Boasting the best graphics 1993 could muster and thumping, bass-driven electronica from both overhead and subwoofer speakers, it cost two quarters per credit and dried out most allowances before players could even escape the first stage. The marquee graphics showed a great black dragon, the colour of deep space, claws extended and maw opened wide to swallow the moon whole, like a delicate yet resilient morsel, just beyond reach. The attract screen, tearing up the monitor, was of the same battle, animated. The player controlled moonbase marshalled their forces, sending flights of disposable defensive missiles out to strike the great wyrm's armour, exploding in a symphony of multi-coloured light. The beast would shriek, shaking the screen and re-aligning the cannons and shields that were humanity's only hope of survival. Then the glimmering dragon would swoop downward like a falling star, talons extended, rending space-suited soldiers limb from limb in bloody relief, breathing a silver fire along the pockmarked surface of the Earth's satellite.

In the end, Bakunawa always devoured the moon, morsel by morsel. No matter how many cannonades were fired, nor how many soldiers gave up their lives bravely in service of the defense of Diana, the dragon always won. He could be deflected, distracted, stunned, and even wounded -- but never killed. At least not so far. Not even by Ricky.

Ricky patted the manager genially on the back as he swept by him, his entourage trailing behind. He walked past the row of pinball machines, a few stray players who didn't buy into the hype pounding at the buttons and swinging their hips into the hard metal, hoping to escape a tilt while recovering a lost ball. To his left a popcorn machine, mounds of exploding kernels flowing from the stainless bucket above to join the rest at the bottom of the bin. Usually stale, Ricky avoided the snack food unless he was feeling particularly lightheaded after a long session or too much to drink.

There was a line-up for Bakunawa, though several eager players waiting in line motioned to defer to Ricky when they wheeled around to see him joining the queue.

"No, no. You go ahead. Game is short anyways. I can wait," he said, smiling graciously. The low light of the arcade cast his face in shadow, his eyes unseen, a mystery.

The kid currently at the controls didn't have a hope in hell. It was clearly his first time playing the game and he didn't seem particularly skilled in the first place. His hand rested awkwardly atop the hard plastic ball of the joystick and his right hand hammered artlessly at the buttons, mashing them out of time. His sprite soldiers did their best in response, launching a full assault of missiles and gunfire at the outer atmosphere. They approached the dragon with increasing velocity, followed by a second fusillade, then a third.

The problem was, Bakunawa was no longer there. He disappeared in a mist, seeing the first volley fly through his immaterial soul into the margins of the screen and from there, into nonexistance. Reappearing for the second wave of the lunar assault, the great lizard raised an armoured wing, shielding itself from the barrage. The speakers boomed with the force of the explosive attack, but the dragon unfurled its guardian wing like a flowing cape, flinging the remnants of the missile strike away like raindrops.

Only the third and final effort of the player remained. The missile banks were empty. The soldiers on the surface of the moon stared upward, their blocky heads immobile, their magazines empty of firepower. The base was defenseless.

Bakunawa spread-eagle, great tail whipping side to side in agitation, powerfully muscled legs and forelimbs at the ready. The area immediately surrounding the dragon began to shimmer, distorting the star-field behind it. A gutteral, primal roar built to a careening shriek, piercing the speakers and the ears of all present, causing some of the younger ones to duck in fear. If the great lizard could smile, it appeared to do so, confidence radiating like the dark, dirty magic it had summoned. A black hole grew in concentric circles from Bakunawa's heart, swallowing the stars, then the missiles, then the phosphorous pixels of gunfire. Scattered and inaccurate as the shots had been, far off target, still they were encapsulated and disappeared.

Then, without warning, the rift closed. All was as it had been before. The stars returned to their rightful place. Bakunawa remained motionless.

Then the same shriek, the similar roar, and the portal sprang open again. This time on the surface of the moon. From the great black expanse, the hail of missiles and small arms fire rained down on the depleted shields and spellbound ground forces of the human defenses. The speakers rumbled death cries and curses buried under a wall of the sounds of a lost war. Then, as abrupt as the attack that had preceded it, came a robotic pronouncement, the sneering tone barely concealed.

YOU ARE DEFEATED! GAME OVER!

A ten count began, and those in line fished in their pockets for the quarters necessary to beat the clock. The next boys in line started to push one another for the right to challenge Bakunawa next. In the end, all of them fell prey to the ruthless difficulty of the game, not a single one managing to defeat the first stage. Through it all, Ricky and his entourage watched in silence. Some of his fans left to find more entertaining pastures, taking up the fight sticks and taunting one another to a head to head match-up. Others moved to the side of the chains in an attempt to get closer to the sound and light spectacle that was the new game on the block, the unbeatable titan.

Loss after loss piled up profits in the coin mechanism as each challenger fell in less than sixty seconds, unable to penetrate the dragon's initial onslaught. The mocking mechanical voice of the arcade machine grated on the nerves of some of the more sensitive children, drowning their frustrated excuses, burying each boy in a sonic cemetary.

Then Ricky stood in front of the huge monitor, his hands resting on the controls. The stick felt natural in his hand. The button placement was perfect. The display was just large enough to fill his vision, the peripherals falling away but still there. The normal shit talk and jokes died down. Every soul present was rapt, intent on seeing how far Ricky would be able to press the game, what new secrets he might reveal to those looking on -- secrets that could be traded for sweets or for reputation on the school playground tomorrow.

Ricky pressed the start button and immediately entered the game. He was the moon and her people. The great destroyer threatened all of that. He would not make the same mistakes as those who came before him. He refused to fire, waiting for Bakunawa to make the first move. Wings unfurled, the wyrm swooped in low, inviting attack. Tracking his prey, and leading the perfect amount, Ricky squeezed off a single missile, then another at an advanced angle.

Deftly dodging the first shot, Bakunawa ran full steam into the second explosive. A scream of bestial pain rattled from the sound system, and a hoarse cheer went up from the ring of boy, four or five deep, jostling each other in a semi-circle in the darkest corner of Starrcade. The energy was palpable, fists were raised in the air in triumph, the spirit of flesh over that of cold programming.

It didn't matter that the second stage was twice as hard, or that Ricky was defeated by the first, almost impossible to spot technique that Bakunawa unleashed unto his defenses, overwhelming them. He'd drawn blood, proven that the beast could be beaten. Flesh could conquer computer chips.

He put his name on the high score list as RKY, coming in eighth out of the default ten, and the only true scorer.

The attract screen returned, front and center, challenging him again.

Ricky, still feeling the high from the adrenaline and the dozens of eyes pinned to his screen, drew another couple of quarters from his pocket and steeled himself for the siege to come.

CHAPTER 04
ROGUELIKE

An hour after he'd entered the steel sarcophagus, Kaine was drenched in sweat and gasping for air. The RETRO random selection had defaulted to survival shooter, and he'd barely cracked the top five. He landed in the circle for payout, coming in fourth, and flashed his bank card at the wireless reader for his deposit. It would pay for this week's habits, at least. Lot fees and park rent were still due, from this month and the last, and Kaine was quite sure he'd have to play and place in another round just to try and push to break even.

The interior of the suicide booth felt claustrophobic. A huge monitor took up most of the space in front of his seat, with a hinged slab that could be brought across the lap for joystick play. On a burnished brass hook to his right hung two heavy gloves and a Blindfold, basic black. Wires snaked about the canopy, screwed down and zip-tied. Small light bars, reflecting upwards, ensconced, gave some sparse illumination.

Kaine had made the mistake of playing on the monitor, a move that had nearly cost him his payday if not his life. He found the Blindfold dreadfully uncomfortable when playing most of the retro games, despite the increased field of view. The pixels and voxels became somehow real to him, adding a primal and urgent note of fear to the proceedings. Fear that could help him survive, or perhaps cost him his life if he played too poorly.

One soul out of every match played publicly would be snuffed out, their low-score a last testament bookending their life. The wagers rolled in, anonymous gamertags and bettor tags flooding the social simulcast chat with their offered odds and statistics sheets. Kaine couldn't help but feel a deep, dark pride at his own numbers, which were infinitesmal on the death-rolls and often paying out very little for landing in the payout. He was the closest thing that the shades and suits that haunted the eSports circuit like vultures had to a sure thing. Though he was rarely sober in his thoughts or deeds, Kaine was at least wise enough to know better than to place his fate in the hands of hastily compiled statistics or in the philosophical nothingness that was the notion of a sure thing. Death was just around the corner every time he accepted a new game contract.

Which is precisely what he did, grasping the Blindfold and wrapping it about his temple, over his open eyes.

The interior of the suicide booth was replaced by a void. There was nothing except a floating, three-dimensional wall of retro text, a slightly italicized system font.

ENTER YOUR NAME, ADVENTURER:

Kaine keyed THRASHR. An homage to the metalhead mythos. Hadn't let him down yet.

YOU ARE CLASSLESS. A CLASS CHOICE WILL

BE PRESENTED TO YOU ... SHOULD YOU SURVIVE THAT LONG.

WELCOME TO ROGUELIKE
DEATH IS PERMANENT
NO RESURRECTIONS
NO SECOND CHANCES
NO GAME IS THE SAME TWICE
DON'T FUCK UP

```
________________________________N________________________________
|________________________  \            W+E    %%%          /________________|
|- - - - - - - - - - - - - -.\ \          S      %        //.- - - - - - - - - - -|
|DS                  |  |\___________________. - .______/||              |
|__ _                |  |\\:::::::::::::::::::|_|:::::::://||        ______|
|__    |`- - - - - - - - -|  |-\\:::::::::::::::::::::::::::://-||- - - - - - - - -`  |  __|
|||| | ==========|  |==\\:::::::::::::::::::::::::://==||==========  |  ||||
|WW| | |. `. | |   \\  __        __  //  ||      .`   |WW|
| | | ||| `.__| |___\\|_|_|  __   |_|_|//___||__.`  .`  |  | |
| | |  |w| |. ===| |=====/|_|_| |  _  |  |_|_|\=====||===   |  |  |  |
|==| | | | | | | |-| |---|| |_|_| | |_| | |_|_| ||---||-|,:| | | | |==|
| | | |=| | | | | | || |   | |_|o| |    || || ||w| | | | | |
| | | | | |_| |___|| |_____|   |_____|   |______||___||_||=| | | | | |
| | | |.' | o |=| |===|| |======================||===||=|| | | o| | | |__|
|__| | | | | | | || || ||  `.| | | | |__|
| | | |-| |---|':           :'|---||-| | | |
| | |  |.` | | //          \\ ||  `. | | |
| | | |.` | | //          \\ ||   `.| | |
| |  .` | | //          \\ ||    `. | |
| |  .`  | |//          \\|| `: |
|____|.'________|_//_________________________\\|______.·|___|
```

You stand in a courtyard. Several stunted hardwoods stretch barren limbs skyward. The path you've taken to arrive here through the forest seems to dissipate at your heels. The dark sorcerer's magic, no doubt. An irregular stone wall forms the perimeter of the courtyard, with a gothic manor house directly ahead. Storage sheds crowd the courtyard, likely for dread servants or human sacrifice. Beaten paths of hardpacked dirt lead off to the east and west.

OBVIOUS EXITS: NORTH, EAST, WEST

Kaine hammered out INV reflexively from the menu of preset commands.

You possess: Leather armour. Leather hat. Small knife. One scroll of dispel magic.

He'd been unlucky with his item draw. One scroll of dispel magic to begin with was a poor starting point. At least the random number generator had seen fit to bless him with a weapon, no matter how basic. He moved east, knowing it was best to try and gain some experience and try to pop some items from outside of the dungeon proper before moving inside, no matter how much he wished to hurry. Haste did not make waste in Roguelike, it spelled death. East felt good to him on a gut level, so he motioned for it to be so.

You move east.

You stand in a cemetery. Though there are many headstones,

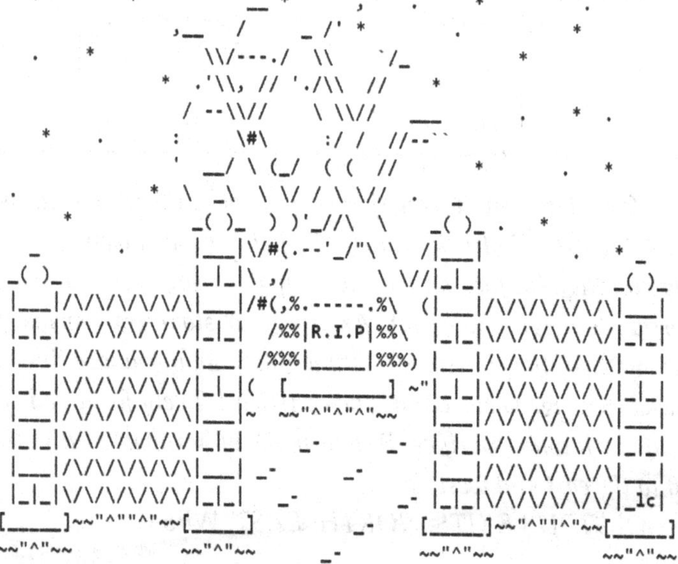

more than a few of them seem to have seen better years. Sagging into the earth, so worn and weathered that they no longer bear inscriptions, they are silent testaments of lives lost. The earth at their granite feet, in many cases, looks recently and suspiciously disturbed.

OBVIOUS EXITS: WEST, EAST.

Two skeletal wretches claw their way to the surface! They face you, undaunted.

Kaine launched his attack, forcing his avatar to tumble forward acrobatically and backstab the first undead before its bones could fully animate against him. The remaining corpse circled about on his character, and though unarmed, it clawed at THRASHR's flesh, doing minor damage through the thick leather armor. He felt, and fought, the urge to scream. His hands deftly worked the buttons to wriggle from their clutches, managing to drive his knife deep into the skull of the abomination, shattering it.

Kaine checked his character sheet reflexively, quickly scanning the numbers.

<THRASHR, HP: 12/14, MP: 0/0, Level 2, Class unassigned>

He'd gained the first level, at least, the experience from the conflict having been enough to give him a bit of a boost. The loss of hit points was worrying this early in the game, but not too distressing.

He ordered his character to root through the inventory of the undead. Nothing of interest. He pressed his avatar onward, east.

You move east.

What once was a small cemetery is now bordering on a turgid, blighted bog. The muck beneath your feet seeks to entrap you [-1 AGI in this zone], allowing your boots to sink into the black earth with abandon. There is a BREACH in the manor walls, here, overgrown with brackish weeds. The wind picks up, howling as it whips across the crevice, bringing with it the salt aroma of rotting vegetation and stillwater vermin.

OBVIOUS EXITS: WEST

Kaine knew better than to trust the obvious dead end, and noted that the word breach was in all caps and coloured a vibrant cyan rather than the simple terminal green and grey that populated most of the Roguelike engine. He compelled his digital flesh to cut away the weeds from the breach.

You begin to hack at the entangled vines that seek to cover the breech in the courtyard walls, your feet slipping deeper into the cold mud as you do so [-2 AGI in this zone].

Kaine held his breath. Now was the perfect time to spring a trap on him, and he knew that the computer behind the wall of text was calculating this very probability. A second later, the floating descriptor moved along, informing him of the result.

The various strands fall away from the harsh cut of your knife. Looking into the small crevasse in the courtyard walls, you spy a filthy rucksack, and an assortment of blackened bones piled up beside it.

THRASHR opens the rucksack. Inside, there is:

a burnished buckler (+2 DEF)

a scroll of detect magic

100 gold coins

Kaine immediately equipped the buckler, instinctively hitting the button to load it from inventory to be worn. His reflexes paid off handsomely.

You hear a shuffling noise behind you. Turning about, and dropping the empty rucksack, you find yourself assaulted by a new foe!

One man o' moss, dark eyes alight with rage, threatens to wrap itself about you and drag you to your death!

THRASHR readied his buckler, keeping his footing on the small bit of solid ground inside the breech, waiting for the lumbering mass of loam and dark magic to attempt the small crevasse.

As soon as the giant mass stuck its head through the crack, THRASHR immediately set to, stabbing it relentlessly into the face and neck of the beast. An unearthly cry erupted from his enemy, and it intensified it's scrabble to get inside, splashing water about and pressing its limbs against the stony sides of the breech in order to gain leverage.

Again and again Kaine instructed THRASHR to attack the monster, knifing it well over a hundred times before it collapsed with a sickening wet sound, like seaweed slapped against a rocky shore by the tide. Such bodies left no room for an inventory, offering mere experience in return for the effort. A summary search of his stats showed he had gained yet another level, and was probably ready to make an approach on the manor. He counted himself fortunate indeed that he did not encounter the man of moss in the bog water, unprotected and bereft of his dexterity.

Quickly navigating back to the courtyard entrance where he had begun the quest, THRASHR set to exploring the NORTH.

You move north.

You stand a the locked gate leading inside the fell magician's mansion. To the EAST and WEST of you stand seemingly abandoned stablehouses and workshops, doors wide open and no candles in the windows. To the NORTH, the locked gate, the portal to a large stone structure emanating an eerie power. You feel shivers down your spine as you gaze in wonder at the evil edifice.

OBVIOUS EXITS ARE: NORTH (LOCKED), EAST, WEST

Kaine knew that searching for the key was often a waste of time, and that the lock could be forced instead. In almost every game of ROGUELIKE he'd played, too many players ended up frantically searching for the key, seeking answers to circular riddles while other players advanced. He ordered THRASHR to attempt to pick the lock.

You attempt to pick the lock, despite not having the correct tools. Inserting the knife edge into the crude tumbler, you hear a grating noise. The lock does not budge. You fail.

Attempt to force the door? Y/N?

Y

THRASHR attempts to barge down the door! The first attempt fails, though the splintering of wood and whining of hinges can be heard. You take 2 points of damage. Attempt again?

Y

THRASHR attempts to barge down the door! The second attempt fails, though the door falls slightly ajar and a dim light can be seen within. You take 2 points of damage. Attempt again?

Y

THRASHR attempts to barge down the door! The door bursts inwards with explosive force! Hinges and screws fall to the stone with a slight ringing noise. You make your way inside.

Kaine checked up on THRASHR's status.

<THRASHR, HP: 14/20, MP: 0/0, Level 3, Class unassigned>

You stand in a dimly lit corridor. Candlelight illuminates very little, but as your eyes adjust to the darkness, you can see a spiral staircase at the far end of the chamber, and a long table long gone to rot. The table is laden with the last meal of those who dined there, obviously many years ago. Bones, dehydrated fruit and vegetables, and the aroma of spoiled wine mingle together to create an unsettling scene. There is a distinct warmth coming from a corridor to the WEST. To the east, yet another barred door. Otherwise, the stairwell appears to be the only open path.

You go WEST.

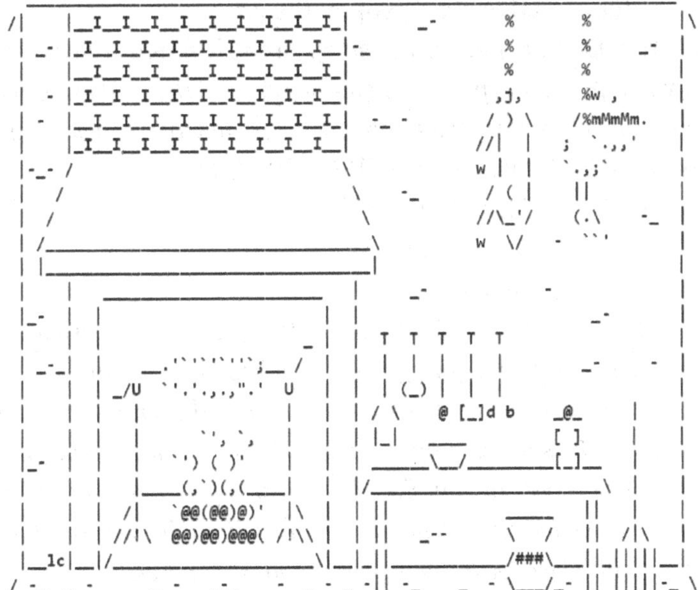

You stand in a well-stocked kitchen. A small roast turns on a spit, unaided by corporeal hands. A large fowl and an even larger vermin hang suspended from meat hooks chained to the ceiling, drained of blood. A small mortar and pestle and a jar of mysterious spice rest next to each other on a small oak table, surface covered with deep knife marks and stained a deep rust. The flame warms the chill from your bones (+2 HP) and ...

A jar bearing a simple and elegant inscription lies beneath the table.

There is a simple broom here, laid against the masonry.

An array of fire-tending tools are hung in a neat row above the table.

Kaine felt a surge of glee at having spotted the jar. Within, he knew, there was a very good chance of a class scroll. To find it this early was also extremely good luck, in the event that it was a class that matched his play style. He ordered THRASHR to open the jar.

You open the jar. Inside there is a small scroll, sealed with wax of a pretty purple shade and wrapped with a ribbon of the same hue. Unfurling the scroll, you immediately feel your powers grow, in the manner of a SPELLSWORD!

You learn Magic Arrow!

You learn Enchant Weapon!

You learn Sootheskin!

<THRASHR, HP: 21/25, MP: 10/10, Level 4, Spellsword>

"Can I help you, young one?" a hollow voice inquires.

You turn about in the kitchen, seeking the source, but see nothing. The spit turning the roast stops in place. Light footsteps move closer to you. Slowly, surely, a gossamer outline in the rough shape of a woman begins to solidify before you. Like spider-silk, she appears transparent and yet tangible at once, the most detail being offered by her face. Cast in a look of deep and unknowable sadness, the ghost reaches out to touch your arm.

Kaine allowed the action to continue despite the risks.

The apparition grazes your forearm, and you are surprised to find it as warm as a human touch. The ghost smiles morosely, then looks away.

"It's been at least a hundred years since I've touched a man. Yet, here you are. Tell me, you are here to slay the master, and to free our spirits?" (Y/N)

Sensing no duplicity from the NPC, Kaine agreed.

Y

The ethereal woman nods, her expression unchanged.

"Then know this, THRASHR. The master lies at the end of a maze, beginning at the top of the staircase. Room after room adjoining, in what seems like an impossibility of size and scope. Take the jar of spices with you, and sprinkle it on the floor as you go. You will never fail to see the route you've already taken, and be free of the maddening influence of the master's magic."

A bit of true joy enters the thin voice of the spirit woman, she gazes at you with milky-white orbs long since deceased.

"He will have no further need of my meals. Of this, I am certain. Farewell, and do not fail."

With that, she fades away, footsteps echoing slightly before being deadened by the walls. The roast, blackened now on one side, began turning on the spit once more. The room is as you entered it.

You take the jar of spice into your inventory.

You move east.

You move upwards.

You stand at the top of the ornate stairwell, a flat quartz resembling marble that reflects the sheen of the full moon as it peers through tall barred windows shot through the mansion. Your shadow creeps across the landing, looming large. There is merely a small wrought-iron table here, bearing a simple vase. Ruby-red roses bend their necks towards you as if curious as to who this intruder could be. There is only one door.

OBVIOUS EXITS ARE: NORTH

Kaine whipped the joystick through his populated inventory, hotkeying the jar of spice, selecting it.

You use the jar of spice. A trail of salt, pepper, and various unknown additives falls to your feet and will trail you wherever you go next.

The next few moments were somewhat harrowing for Kaine despite the use of the mundane jar for a magical purpose. Each room he entered after the first resembled one another, a plain table and a nondescript vase filled with roses in the corner of each. At times, taking random passages, he felt like he was quickly getting lost despite his nigh-eidetic memory. He was building a textual map with his mind as he progressed, augmented by the trail of seasoning that he'd left in his wake. Like a hedge maze with more class and greater urgency, he continued plowing through the options like a madman possessed.

Eventually, after nearly twenty minutes of fruitless labour, THRASHR bested the maze, emerging from the perfectly mirrored mansion rooms into a damp expanse of pitch black. Organ music, wheezing with exertion like old lungs, filled Kaine's ears.

You stand before a cauldron, and a wizened man attending it. You sense that this is the master of this mournful palace. His beard is long and unruly, tumbling down to cover neck and breast. Long, gnarled fingers reach over overtop the bubbling brew that rests within the hot iron pot at his feet, a rank miasma filling the room, sickening you [-1 STR]. He has, as yet, failed to *notice your presence, embroiled in his sorcery.*

THERE ARE NO OBVIOUS EXITS.

Kaine rapped the joystick and pressed the button corresponding to THRASHR's scroll of detect magic.

Stepping forward from the shadows, you unfurl the scroll of detect magic, and read the words inscribed verbatim.

NIHIL NOVE SUB SOLE

With this, the parchment flares up in a pillar of fire and acrid smoke, then is gone. You are now aware of the fact that:

This magic-user is capable of casting: Magic Arrow, Rock Risoluto, Shield Against Steel.

Kaine smiled beneath his Blindfold. He was prepared for this. It would be a tough battle at such a low level, but if he was simply aggressive enough, and waited for just the right moment ...

"Halt, intruder!" the Master intones, ceasing the theatrical wriggling of his fingers. He observes THRASHR with a severe yet thoughtful expression.

"Have you come to try your hand? To attempt what so many souls who have tread before you have attempted to do, failing, wagering their eternal life in the process?" the Master continued, the red-hot glow of the cauldron showing his long robes to be the blue-black of the endless galaxy.

"Don't you know that this is my domain? My realm? My mansion? My home?!" he thundered, at last, his eyes aflame with enchantment.

Kaine didn't waste any time trying to negotiate with the end boss, knowing that it would cost him time and the element of surprise. Instead, he ordered THRASHR to cast Magic Arrow, silently. It would cost more magic points, but he had but one remaining use for those. He gripped the joystick and placed his fingers at the ready, moving forward.

THRASHR casts Magic Arrow under his breath! Otherwordly lances streak from his fingers to pierce the Master! The Master reels in pain, stumbling backwards.

You close the distance between the two of you.

The Master recovers, his face the definition of fury. He retaliates, replying in kind with his own Magic Arrows! They strike THRASHR dead on! [-6 HP].

THRASHR attempts a backstab, circling The Master. He succeeds, planting the dagger deep into his victim's back! The Master staggers free, flailing with abandon. Screams of rage accentuated by the power of the beyond echoes throughout the darkened chamber.

The Master, bleeding freely, begins whispering to the shadows. A translucent bubble forms about him, protecting him from the outside world. From the very flagstones at their feet, hands of stone emerge, grasping for THRASHR's ankle.

You are caught! You are immobile!

Kaine cursed under his breath, redoubling his efforts, hands a blur now.

THRASHR cuts viciously against the rocky bonds threatening to crush his feet. Meanwhile, an additional flight of silver streaks slams into your torso, dealing an additional [-6 HP] of damage.

You manage to free yourself.

Kaine knew it was all or nothing with his next move. He spent the rest of his remaining mana.

THRASHR's blade becomes engulfed in bright blue flame, turning translucent in the process!

THRASHR's blade passes through the Master's bar-

rier, cutting deep into the Master's neck!

THE MASTER IS SLAIN!

The brightly coloured bubble disappears, the chamber is once more plunged into a near-perfect darkness. The bulky robes of the dead wizard cushion his body as he falls to the stone floor.

Kaine pumped his fist in the air and let out an excited whoop as he awaited the results of his victory over the forces of evil, nearly knocking off his Blindfold.

There was still fifteen minutes remaining before the time limit of one hour ran out. Kaine groped around, still blind, for his box of beer. Finding it where he left it near the seat of the suicide booth, he cracked a cold one and took a few satisfying drinks.

Then words, like buildings, stood tall and proud in front of him. A dramatic flourish of brass and woodwind proclaimed the end of this session of the game.

GAME OVER

ROGUELIKE CLAIMS ITS VICTIMS

Those who failed to garner any bonus points during the adventure: 10

Those who died outside the manor: 34

Those who died in the kitchen and sitting room: 19

Those who died in the maze of the mansion: 26

Those who died fighting the master and his servants: 10

Those who survived the quest: 1

PAYOUT:

THRASHR

ENCIN0

NIGHTMAN

YGRITTE

ALGERNON

LO-SCORE: Sisyphus
HI-SCORE: THRASHR

Kaine beamed from ear to ear, leaning back against the sticky metal of the booth and just letting the ambiance of the moment move over him. It was a brief and unusual moment of peace for the old man. It was also a triumph for him. He won. Sisyphus lost. Someone had to.

Kaine tried not to think of the poor bastard, sitting somewhere either a block or a world away. It was a big nation, after all, and anyone could sit in those seats. Games didn't discriminate.

At least it would be peaceful. Sisyphus, his screen name obscuring the empathy evoked by his real one, would just go to sleep. And he'd never wake up.

CHAPTER 05
TAKE THE LONG WAY HOME

The entrance to the trailer park was a depleted mess, rusting chainlink fence falling free of from the posts and a handpainted sign declaring it home to five hundred unfortunate souls. Old shipping containers repurposed to provide shelter and ancient mobile homes huddled together, barely a handspan apart, rotten verandahs melding together into an unholy design.

Kaine clutched the last bottle of Baron in his hand, just the dregs at the bottom left. He was sweating bullets from the walk home, his limp impossible to mask despite his self-medication.

He strolled into the land-lease community (for this was what the government termed the tenements) with shoulders slumped and a deep hurt inside despite his victories. The money he'd made might be enough to stave the wolves away from the door for a month or maybe more -- but they'd be back, howling in the recesses of his mind, threatening to claim him as they always did.

The makeshift shelters were painted a variety of bright hues, an expression of what little agency the people here had left. Canary yellow faded to an aquamarine splattered across the side of a rusted through currogated container. Graffiti sprawled across a bowed mobile home that had to be nearing a century old, a raised fist clutching a crude branch. But the most common artistic theme was neglect and depression, great raised canker sores of rust and rot that was a commonality across all of the domiciles.

Kaine eventually stopped in front of his own castle, a turn of the millenia model mobile that had been feature rich and well-maintained in its heyday. No longer. It served as a place to sleep, eat, and very rarely fuck. Ever since he'd turned sixty, Kaine hadn't had the natural vigor of his youth to supplement and suppress the nagging existential fear in his heart necessary to do the deed properly. His looks faded, as did Rebecca's. Their sons, fully grown, were only a paper-thin wall away. The sexual math was written in bold, and so he took little interest in that compact of their aging marriage. What little was left of it was something he still held sacred, even if she didn't.

The lights were on. Rebecca was up, likely polishing off a handle of rye before bed. Some habits were shared between them, and in this, they had a strange kinship that transcended the formal vows of matrimony. Addiction and escape made comfortable bedfollows, even when old maids and bitter misanthropists no longer shared the same bed.

Old christmas lights were strung, criss-crossed like bandoliers holding broken bullets, across the entire facade of his trailer. The bulbs that survived dared give off their incandescent light, bold blues and greens and reds and oranges. His neighbours teased him about the festive nature of the artistic statement, but deep down, everyone appreciated the warmth it afforded. Faded tin tavernalia was pop-riveted into place amongst the lights, giving the impression that his place was something of a speakeasy, which it was on weekends. Many of his neighbours would congregate on Friday, or Saturday, or nigh any other night of the week to down some of their favourite liquors on his deck or on the small scrap of dead grass he called his front lawn.

The rain had reached a crescendo and he was thoroughly soaked as he stomped up onto the deck and threw the door open. He was immediately greeted by the buzzing warmth of the space heater set up on the kitchen counter and scent of tobacco smoke, mingled with marijuana. His wife, face painted on and long nails clutching a spliff, stared back at him from the fold-out kitchen table. Her other hand was wrapped around the neck of a tall bottle of rye, as he'd predicted. The amber liquid it had once contained was nearly gone. Hey eyes were glassy, wide open, yet vacant.

The interior of his home wasn't much better than what was presented on the outside. A popsicle-stick cross hung crooked from a thumbtack above the kitchen table, his concession to his wife's professed faith. Old movie posters from the 80s and 90s, mostly martial arts action pieces, were pinned to the cheap prefab walls, breaking up the beige monotony. Fake ferns in dollar store pots were placed on the cracked vinyl flooring, never requiring water and thus only showing their neglect via the thick coat of dust adorning their fronds.

"Out late, lover?" Rebecca slurred, taking another puff

off the spliff, eyes slits.

"Yeah. Out gaming. Making some cash," Kaine replied.

"Good. Maybe some day your ass won't come back."

Kaine snorted at the cheap shot and casually tossed his empty beer into the blue box.

"Yeah, like I haven't heard that before."

"And you'll hear it again," his wife promised, trying hard to keep her eyes open.

"... and again and again and again. You're like a broken record Becca. I just tune that shit out, you know?"

"That's a two way street, honey." Rebecca lost her battle with her eyelids and her head drooped, her neck unable to support the weight.

Kaine walked to the fridge, a faded yellow stalwart that had seen the better side of two decades of service. A loud hum emanated from the rear, echoing against the gyprock, adding a bass note to the cheap tin notes from the clock radio churning out old country set on the stovetop.

"Hoping for some Johnny again, were you?" Kaine asked idly, bent over, feeling the knots in the muscles of his back, fishing for a cold one.

"'Bout the only cash I can expect around this shithole, that's for damn sure." Rebecca coughed, hacked, then wheezed with laughter, the ash from her smoke falling loose onto the tabletop. There was a moment where the silence was only punctuated by the treble ringing of the knock-off radio murmuring a saccharine love ballad.

"... how much did you win tonight?"

"Two grand. Top tier in the first game, first place in Roguelike," Kaine said, finally finding his bottle and straightening with an audible crack in his spine. He groaned, then grimaced, then cracked the cap off. It had been a long day -- first, a full shift slinging ewaste and then a few high-stakes games. And he had to wake up before noon and do it all over again.

"Two grand? That's enough to pay down my credit!" Rebecca exclaimed. She tried to stand up and fell to the side, tumbling out of the fold out chair onto the floor. Kaine moved to help her but she batted his hands away viciously, cursing.

"I don't need your goddamn help, Ricky! I can get up on my own," she said. First, hands and knees, and then, woozily, she gained her footing and stood erect. She brushed off her thin pink blouse and shook her head from side to side. "See?"

"Yeah. It's enough to pay off the credit. But only half of it's going there. I'm keeping the other half. Some for the kids, and some for myself."

She tried to slap him, seemingly out of nowhere. Yet he was ready, raising his arm to block the clumsy strike. Her forearm collided against his and didn't budge an inch. Years of manual labour and his own quick reflexes had saved him many times from her attempted abuse. He laughed while she seethed.

"So fucking predictable. Now you're not getting a dime, and the kids are getting your share. I'm going to put it in a trust for them, sole beneficiaries. Remember that the next time you try to get a cheap shot in on me."

By now his wife was sobbing, saccharine, the usual. There was not a nook in the depths of Ricky Kaine's heart that was not hardened to her. Crocodile tears spurred on by heavy intoxication rolled from the corners of her dull blue eyes and down her painted cheeks. She looked like a weathered porcelain doll, one of the ones Ricky's grandmother had collected in neat rows in her guest room. It was a strange memory for the moment, but it served.

"Cry all you want. It's not changing a thing. Maybe if you apologize and sober up I'll change my mind about the next score," Ricky said, softly but firmly. His eyes never left her face, just in case he saw any nastiness return to her.

"I'm going to bed," Rebecca replied in between great heaves and hiccups. She smoothly palmed the handle of liquor and pulled it tight against her blouse as she brushed past him. There, Kaine knew, she'd pass out within minutes, her wallscreen turned on to one of the gossip streams.

"Good night," he said. There was no reply, just the shuffle of her footsteps down the narrow hallway that led to the bathroom and the family bedrooms.

Then he was alone. He knew that Marcus and Tilly were likely either in their own bedrooms, asleep or gaming, or gone entirely, hitting the skids downtown somewhere. He loved both of his children but was never sure if they loved him back, despite the father's day and birthday ecards he was sure to get every second or third year. Disrespect was de jure in his household and yet it was the only place where Kaine felt comfortable. The irony did not escape him.

He turned to the small, open concept living room that shared the space with the kitchen, a small slatted half-wall all that seperated the two. Unlike the kitchen, the living room was carpeted, a thick brown shag that had been on sale ten years ago and had reminded him once again of the small country bungalow he'd often visit where his grandparents lived. Nearby there had been a deep muddy river that his grandfather would often take him to on sunny days to fish, their lines shining against a bright blue sky. Here, it rained almost all of the time under constant cloud cover, and the dampness seemed a permanent fixture.

The walls of the living room shared some of the adornments of the kitchen, action heros grimacing over lethal black hardware, bright bold titles emblazoned near the bottom of the wrinkled posters. A few family photographs were mixed in between, cheap frames collecting dust and mold. There was the day Marcus was born, Rebecca as red as a lobster, and the both of them beaming as she held the newborn swaddled near to her heart. He'd had a fine beard then. Next to it, the day Tilly joined the family and made them complete. Marcus was old enough to stand beside the hospital bed, his small hand on the sullied sheets, looking away from the camera as he and his wife welcomed their daughter into the world. Those smiles faded over time, as did the colours of the photograph. He'd never bothered to convert them to digital file formats. When they were gone, they were gone.

The Blindfold was laid haphazardly on the small, simple coffee table adjacent to the sofa. The charge cable was plugged into the Blindfold, snaking around the leg of the coffee table and up over the beaten down pillows of the couch, then finding its way to the nearest USB port. A pale white light emanated from beneath the velveteen cloth wrapped about the visor, gently pulsing.

Kaine padded into the living room and continued sipping at his beer. He flopped down into the couch cushions and spread eagled, throwing his head to rest on the back of the sofa, letting out a great sigh. It was nearly silent. Seconds ticked away as Kaine closed his eyes and tried to recenter himself, tried to block out all of the extraneous thoughts that came prodding into his waking consciousness. He didn't even open his eyes to finish his drink, putting it down without thought.

He opened his eyes only to lean forward, placing the empty bottle on the coffee table. Kaine unplugged the Blindfold from the charge cable and wrapped it tight about his temples, pressing the power button for a few seconds before lying down.

The white light in his eyes intensified, then showed him a dazzling array of coloured rays whisking about in full dimension and definition. The surround sound speakers located at the cusp of his ear canal chimed in perfect tune, welcoming him to the network. His transition from the outside world was complete. He would proceed wherever he looked, controlling the narrative with the muscles of his eyes and eyelids, almost second nature after years of practice. Panels displaying the latest news cohabitated a virtual backsplash beside mountains of advertising, each product thrust so close that Kaine could almost touch them. Perfectly tuned to his tastes, alcohol ads butted up against coupons for cheap fast food less than a ten minute walk from the entrance to the trailer court.

He allowed his eyes to rest on one of his favourite streams -- let's play. From the Atari era through to the eight and sixteen bit systems and beyond, rendered in post-processed 3D. Kaine had a few favourite content creators and settled on allowing the Blindfold to choose at random for him, ogling the random button for just long enough to click. Then, the white light faded to black, then centered a pixellated portrait in front of his eyes, alone.

Kaine fell asleep to the sound of chiptunes whispering into his ears.

CHAPTER 06
WORK, OR WHAT IS LEFT OF IT

The picking shed was hot as hell. Kaine was sweating buckets in his thick overalls, though the black fabric prevented any stains from showing through. Large cage fans attached to the walls blew fetid air about the large hangar, the few windows covered with old bedsheets to prevent most of the sunlight from penetrating. The room reeked of burning metal and plastic, the thin paper masks fitted tight around the worker's mouths doing little to mitigate the foul odour.

He'd just come off a half hour lunch break and had already spotted a few choice pieces that he'd managed to secret away in his pockets. He usually bought a few rounds of beer for the supers on the weekends at the local watering hole to ensure that his cargo pockets didn't get the patdown on the after-shift inspection. A few nice RAM sticks, a couple of CPUs minus heatsinks -- too bulky to hide effectively -- and even a near-mint solid state drive. All in all, worth a couple of hundred dollars by the time he slotted them into systems and sold them secondhand. Picking and flipping was a part-time job for Kaine, something besides gaming that could help to bring whatever money he could to pay for a roof over his family's head.

He was currently digging through a plastic wastebin filled with parts. Grimy wiring and bent pin connectors clashed together, scraping bits of errant metal off with every adjustment he'd make. Boards with lots of components intact were kept; his job was to find the absolute scrap and pull it loose onto the factory floor before moving on to the next. The thin gloves with rubberized grip he was issued at the start of every shift rarely lasted to the end, thick callouses from years of service had inured him to the pain of the sharp edged electronics and pinpricks of random bits of debris. Most workers discarded the gloves by lunchtime in favour of bare hands in any cases, fingers clammy and wrinkled from the condensation.

Large, retro monitors -- likely salvaged from the bins themselves -- were hung by thick chains to the steel trusses above. Each real time image dissolved into the next, a panaramo of labour effort, displaying each employees bin number, pick proficiency, and overall speed. Slack too much and your name would highlight red, and your pay would immediately begin being docked in direct tune with the pace of your picking. Fail to strip a board that you missed at the bottom of the bin and that too would be indexed under your name as the hundreds of employees scrolled by. Like the televised stock tickers that Kaine remembered when he was young, only this time it was human life that was being indexed and tracked rather than invisible and intangible stocks. There was no performance bonus for being faster than required.

The hours bled free. Monotony let his mind wander.

Pattern recognition. Odds. Percentages. Damages per second. Hit points. Hitboxes. Counting frames. Spellbooks. Ship specifications. The metagame. What mattered.

"Associate Kaine," a super called out to him from behind a full gas mask. Supers got a few perks, much like the field overseers of rural labour farms. Bought loyalty. Kaine turned away from his bin, though his hands kept working at invisible tasks.

"Yeah?"

"Adjunct wants to have a word with you. You're officially on stasis. You can leave your bin," a gruff voice growled through the mask. Kaine tried to size the man up, but he found that he was clearly unfamiliar with this super. Not one of the guys Kaine was friendly with on the downshift, that was for certain.

A replacement worker, also a face behind a mask that Kaine didn't recognize, immediately brushed past the old man and started working on the bin wordlessly. Kaine checked the monitor to make sure his name was black-bordered, showing him to be on sanctioned break. He wasn't going to any meetings he wasn't getting paid for. He'd put up with this dead-end drudgery for decades and was tired of the shit.

Still, he reminded himself as he squared his shoulders, aging muscles aching with a deep burn, it could always be worse.

"This way, associate," the super ordered, lifting a big arm pointing to the adjuncts tower. Placed squarely in the center of the factory floor, the room on stilts rose above even the monitors, threatening to scrape the thin tin roof of the repurposed hangar. Forest green paint, laid on thick, peeled unevenly on the silts, giving them a strange camouflage appearance. A wide steel staircase was riveted to the stilts, hugging each turn and angle, leading to the very top.

The super followed a few feet behind him, and even unarmed, it felt like a prison style procession. Kaine climbed the stairs, one foot in front of the other, his good hand on the guiderail. Looking down on the shop floor, his coworkers looked like ants, milling away, industrious and anonymous in their travails. Nearing the top, his muscles sore from all of the last night's walking and the general malaise of the years, Kaine paused for a stretch.

"Problem sir? Move along please." the super said. He hadn't even waited for a response to the question before moving on to the command. The very model of empathy, Kaine thought to himself, a smirk spreading across his face.

"Sorry, my man. A little sore. An old man's curse, you know?" Kaine replied, turning his head to try and catch the eyes behind the small dark circles of the gas mask. Seeing nothing, but feeling an urgent tension between them, Kaine returned to his climb and quickly gained the landing.

The door in front of him was solid looking wood, painted in the same emerald hue that the stilts had been. It was a nice, soft contrast against the nondescript grey that was the default colour of the prefab building that was the adjunct's office. Beside the door, a long, narrow window the wound about the entirety of the tower in a full panorama. The window allowed easy visual surveillance of any worker on the floor. A fact that was subconsciously absorbed by most of the peasants below almost as soon as they started their first shift with the eWaste Division, and never forgotten.

"Well, what are you waiting for? Open up and go inside. Adjunct Logan will be extremely displeased as it is given how long it took you to get here. Time is money, associate. Time is valuable."

Kaine didn't reply, deigning merely to co-operate while gritting his teeth with all of the filthy curses he could dredge up into memory. He turned the doorknob and pushed the wooden door open, hobbling inside. He felt the super at his back, taking a few steps forward, then pulling the door closed behind him.

Kaine was alone with the adjunct. Despite having allegedly left the age of paper behind decades ago, file folders in an array of weak pastel colours were piled messily on nearly every available surface. The floor was littered with stacks of paperwork, leaning towards that threatened to break free and spill their faded beige contents all over. Above the surveillance window, running parallel and also spanning the entire perimeter of the room, were arrays of flat panel displays. Pixellated surveillance footage from old drones was fed into some of them, others reflected the same productivity matrix as was being shown to the workers themselves. A few stray monitors played international news feeds, text tickers telling the top stories that today had to offer -- volume muted.

The adjunct, wearing his usual oversized black suit, was slung over an armchair, idly smoking a cigar. The air filtration system attached to the ceiling ducts pulled the coils upwards, yet the aroma remained. For a few beats neither man said anything, simply staring at one another. Then the adjunct, a heavyset man with a thin moustache, sat upright with a groan and tapped an inch of ash into a shallow brass bowl on the dark oak desk. Aside from a small tablet, it was the only ornamentation of any kind in the room.

"Aren't you afraid you'll light the place on fire with that habit?" Kaine risked a joke, reading the man he'd worked under but never spoken to for the twenty odd years he'd worked here.

The adjunct laughed, a short bark that faded into a rumble. Kaine realized he didn't know the fat man's name. He also realized that the adjunct almost certainly didn't care to know Kaine's name, pulling it from the records like any other number.

"Funny old bastard, aren't you? Most of the kids that get the long walk up into this tower piss their pants before they even open their mouths. But not you, right?"

Kaine didn't take the bait, just shifted uncomfortably and shrugged his shoulders.

"No, not you," the adjunct growled, smirking. He put the cigar to his lips and blew a huge ring of smoke that burst against Kaine's breast, spreading out over his overalls.

"Listen, Kaine. You've done some good work here. Almost always on time, sometimes hung over -- not that that shows on all of these fancy charts they have me compile on the daily -- and your productivity year-over-year is in the top fifth despite your age."

Kaine waited for the other shoe to drop.

"But a few things have come to my attention in recent

weeks. Items of interest that I had to investigate, taking such things very seriously."

Kaine put his weight on his good leg now, feeling a sinking dread fill the pit of his stomach.

"Empty your pockets, would you?" the adjunct asked, raising an eyebrow and once more reclining in his deep seat. The cherry of his cigar burned brightly as he puffed at it, his eyes locked onto Kaine's face.

Kaine plunged his fists into his pockets, then withdrew them, empty.

"You got me, boss. But I'm not the only one that takes a few old bits and pieces now and again. Half the goddamn factory floor takes some of the gear home. You know this. It's not news to you," Kaine rasped, his grey eyes narrowing in anger.

"It is news to me, former associate Kaine. And I'm not concerned with the rest of your ex-coworkers. I'm concerned with you and your behaviour. I said to empty your pockets. That wasn't a request."

"Fuck you. If you're going to fire me anyways, I'm keeping the shit." Kaine spat, turning away from the adjunctly abruptly and reaching for the door. It opened before he could do so and the super whom had escorted him here stepped forward, knocking him back.

"Empty your pockets sir, or you'll be charged with theft," the adjunct crowed, barely concealing his delight in humiliating the old man.

Kaine fished through this pockets, then threw the spare parts violently against the front of the desk, breaking at least one of the RAM sticks in two.

"Oh my, Mr. Kaine. Such a horrible temper. You do

realize that those scraps weren't worth more than an hour of your time, let alone a minute of mine?"

Kaine leaned over the desk and spit directly in the adjunct's face, a great string of saliva creeping over the cigar and extinguishing it.

"Jesus Christ! Supervisor Cleary, round up this animal and get him the fuck out of here! You just cost yourself your severance package, Kaine! Disgusting!" the adjunct spit out his cigar and wiped at his face and neck with small, chubby hands.

"Out! Out! Out!" were the last words Kaine heard before rough fingers grasped at his frail body and pushed him hard out the door. He stumbled and fell hard against the railing, feeling the stairs sway ever so slightly in their moorings.

"Get moving, Kaine. You heard the man. Your ass is fired. I'm taking you to the gate and then I don't want to see your sorry ass here again. Ever."

The man in the gas mask had a note of deadly intent in his voice. He'd known what was about to happen even before leading Kaine up those stairs the first time.

"Cleary, who the hell sold me out? Who brought it up the chain to the adjunct? Was it Wilson? Deckard? Layton?" Kaine tried to crane his neck around to speak to the super, but got a quick jab to the ribs for his trouble. Grunting in pain, and with no response forthcoming, Kaine sighed and got back to limping down the stairwell, then through the factory floor. Some of his former friends and coworkers raised their faces to him, eyes speaking their regrets. Most of them kept their focus on their work, unwilling or simply not wanting to meet his gaze. They might be next was the thought on most of their minds.

In a matter of minutes the two man procession had cleared the factory floor, exited the huge doors at the rear, and stood baking in the noonday sun. A small guard-post operated by a robotic enforcer and a sliding chain-link fence were all that seperated them from the outside world.

The fence slid open noiselessly. Kaine could feel the gravel beneath his feet shift and crunch as he took a few steps forward.

"Remember what I said Kaine. I see you nosing around here again, you're dead. Be my pleasure," Cleary threatened.

Kaine let the words fall behind him, as if he hadn't heard them. He pulled his aviators out of his pocket and out them on, leaning back. He stared at the city skyline in the distance, imagining all the lives that had been snuffed out under the simple and impersonal justice of massified life.

Snorting, then spitting once more to his right, he limped away from the worksite, the bright blue sky swallowing him whole.

CHAPTER 07
BOYHOOD

Ricky was poking around some soft seahorse shaped macaroni dinner in his bowl, bored out of his skull. He'd been grounded after his parents had heard about him bullying some of the kids at the arcade out of their quarters. In reality, he'd just beaten them so badly that they couldn't handle the shame, and had pumped their own quarters into the coin slot to be whipped again and again. His parents didn't understand video games, arcades, or the subculture itself and so took the complaint at face value. His consoles had been unhooked, stored in the closet, and locked under guard and key.

The entertainment options outside of the electronics in the trailer were sorely lacking from the teenager's perspective. A slim bookshelf stood in the corner, sagging shelves filled with old issues of Cosmopolitan and Reader's Digest, a few old westerns and romance novels mixed in haphazardly. They hadn't been disturbed in quite some time, the entire fixture approaching ornamental status. Thin cobwebs arced away from the shallow slopes of the bookshelf and attached themselves to the floral wallpaper that bounded the paneled ceiling.

His father was passed out on the sofabed, an eight pack of cans crumpled and strewn across the coffee table. He was snoring loudly, drowning out the daytime talk show host who was trying to get their guest to admit to a shocking paternity test result. Ricky didn't watch much TV, and even less talk show garbage, but he had to admit a certain fondness for the trickery and scripted emotion that went into the performances. His mother was out working at the local fast food joint, scheduled on drive thru. Sometimes his friends would joke about how she served them a hot mess. Sometimes his friends got punches in their snide little faces. Ricky didn't take shit inside or outside of his stomping grounds.

No stranger to being grounded, Ricky pushed his bowl away and stood up, padding kitten-quiet to put his shoes on, by the front door. Arcade opened in thirty minutes, just enough time to get away before the old man woke up a few hours later and realized his son had gone missing. He slipped his sneakers on, already laced, and opened and closed his front door with the agility of a trained thief. His bike was still tied up to the ramshackle shed they had in their lot, a tiny little affair that was held together with baling twine and a liberal application of deck spikes. Finding his shades clipped into the neck of his t-shirt, he unhinged them and put them on, appreciating the dark clarity they offered against the overbearing orb above. Ricky then pocketed his portable CD player and slipped the cans over his ears, unlocking his bike and jumping astride.

The summer breeze felt warm against his skin as he

took off down the dirt road, flanked by tall stands of trees on either side as he exited the driveway. He lived deep in the county and it was nearly a half hour bike ride to town. During the journey he was sure to see cornfields belonging to various family farms, pastures full of grazing cattle and proud, tall horses. A few cars, rusted and with mismatched doors and rims, bucked past him, kicking up great twisters of dust in their wake. Some of them honked their horns at Ricky as they moved aside to pass, old man Winston even daring a wave at the youngster he often served at the ice cream counter in the mall, just a few shops down from the arcade.

The pastoral milieu, like the meandering river that ran alongside some portions of the road, faded into the town proper. The trees ceased their wild randomness and became arranged plots, looming large over cultivated laneways and public thoroughfares. Small wooden houses painted bright pastels sat neatly next to one another. Corner stores with creaking, handpainted signs did brisk business. Mainstreet had a few pubs, a grocery store, and a two-screen theatre where the latest action movie sat next to a children's feature almost every night.

The mall sat almost in the dead center of town. A small parking lot with freshly painted lines corraled the mall, instantiating its own space. Low bushes, clipped into neat squares, sprouted beautiful pink and red roses.

A group of young punks familiar to Ricky had formed around the corner from the main doors of the mall, milling about and passing around a smoke. They called him over as he locked up his bike to the rack and strode towards the entrance.

"Ricky! Hey, Ricky!" a spritely looking girl with bright pink hair cried out to him, a butt smoldering in between her thumb and forefinger.

He adjusted his trajectory to join them in the corner, away from the breeze. Lots of fistbumps and friendly slurs were tossed about as introductions. The pixie girl, her name escaping Ricky for the moment, made a motion to pass him the smoke. He waved it off politely. She smirked.

"Are you sure, Rick? After today's news I thought you might need one."

That certainly piqued his interest. He turned to look at her, squinting.

"News? I've been grounded all day."

A chorus of laughter and boos rang out against the faded brickwork of the shopping center as the mallrats teased and taunted him loudly. His scowl deepened.

"Ricky, it's a joke, not a dick. Don't take it so hard," a disheveled looking stoner Ricky didn't know jibed, chuckling over his cigarette.

"Just tell me what's up, and I won't beat the piss out of you. How's that for a deal?" Ricky was tired of the sniggering and squared his shoulders against the stoner.

"Arcade's closed. Last day was today," pixie girl interjected, attempting sympathy. She reached out and touched his arm. He didn't feel a thing.

"What?" Ricky heard himself say.

"Yeah. Arcade's done for. Not enough business and lots of parents were complaining to town council about the bad influence it was having on the younger kids. The usual bullshit, you know?"

The stoner, dropping his smoke, knelt to grab it while talking. His tar-stained fingertips probed the grass and gravel looking for the remnants.

Ricky didn't hear the rest of the conversation -- he was already on his way through the mall doors and headed down to Starrcade. Everything appeared as usual for a sunny afternoon in the sleepy community. The shoe store, the outlet clothing store, and the jeweler's were all doing brisk business in anticipation of proms, weddings, and honeymoons. The food court, fast food chains stacked in side by side with mom and pop's deep fried cuisine, bustled with youth, their backpacks slung sloppily onto tables and over the backs of chairs.

Down in the corner, dead black, with merely Mr. Starr standing outside fussing about the intricate neon tubes above the entrance, lied the last arcade in a hundred miles. The machines had been turned off. The usual ringing and bleeping was replaced with a dull buzz of conversation. Ricky caught up with the owner as he stood, arms folded, contemplating the universe as he stared at the gaseous artwork that had announced to the world that this was a safe space, a place of youthful exuberance, a congregation of misfits and castaways who had made this place their mecca.

"Ah, Ricky. I'd expected you earlier," Starr said, turning away from his thoughts to face the teenager. His face was carved from stone, a downcast and depressing cast etched deeply into the pores and lines of his age-spotted skin.

"I was grounded, Mr. Starr. But this!" Ricky gesticulated wildly at the dead cabinets and the empty countertop where coins had once been handed back for bills. He had no more words.

"Yes. Hard to believe it myself. This place opened up in the late seventies. Fifteen years later, here we are. Did you know I used to work here full-time, just to keep the place running?" Starr reminisced, returning his eyes to the sign with a far-away look. His mind travelled the years spanning then to now, a thousand memories dredged up in between. Ricky shared many of them, and had his own. For some time, neither said a word.

"But why? This place was busy almost every day of the week?"

"Times change, Ricky. Lots of pressure from the municipal government on this one. Said punks and underage kids were wasting their lives here and picking up some bad habits. Hard to argue against that type of conjecture. This is a church-loving community, Ricky. Video games and kids playing hooky go together hand in hand. And when they come home smelling like smoke and greasy food, those types of parents are going to go after my head."

"Fuck them, then!" Ricky spat out bitterly. He could feel tears springing to his eyes. He knuckled them away savagely. Ricky felt a large warm hand rest on his shoulder. Starr had turned away once again, this time, all of his attention was focused on the boy.

"Ricky, I'm not your father, so I'll overlook the language. I understand why you're so angry. I'm upset myself. This was something that I built myself and a place where people could come and enjoy themselves, a little escape from the rest of the world. You and I both know that not everyone is cut out for hunting and fishing and riding a beat-up four-wheeler down the back roads. Some of the local kids like yourself take a bit from both worlds. But a lot of the ones I saw here had nothing else. Some of those kids are your friends. Almost all of them are mine. You think this doesn't hurt me?"

Ricky wept, then, covering it with his forearm. Starr squeezed his shoulder gently. Between the tears, and beneath the flickering neon, the marquee for Bakunawa glimmered in his eyes, the shooting star and the silver dragon dancing in his mind's eye from that moment forward.

CHAPTER 08
A GLITCH IN TIME

University was a small cinderblock room with ethernet cables hanging like garter snakes hanging above the cots. It was the smell of salsa and cheap corn chips, stale beer and cold pizza. For Ricky, it was a great time in his history of gaming.

In the far corner of his shared room, a small 8 by 11 slot in a stone dormitory built a century ago, Ricky hammered away at his online opponents. The high-pitched clicks of his mouse were so quick as to be uncountable, switching perspective and launching macros all at once. His hands flew over the keys of the mechanical keyboard like a virtuoso pianist, perfect flow.

There was a conversation going on about him, in his periphery, but he could only pick out bits and pieces. His mind was acutely focused on the match at hand, everything else incidental. The treble of guitar strings could be heard, voices singing crudely and out of tune beyond the rubber padding of his headset.

He was conducting a siege against an opposing tribe in the latest dark fantasy MMO, Darkhorse. Unlike the most popular games like it at the time, the in-game politics were a serious affair and player-built cities and castles meant land and resources and spawns were always up for grabs. Trebuchets were being build by polygonal peasants, blocky hands hoving aimlessly over the siege engines. Slightly more impressively textured soldiers flooded either side of the wooden constructs, rushing to meet the castle walls -- walls that were already cracked and broken from the heavy stone hailstorm. Swords, pikes, crossbows, and spears were held aloft in irregular animations as they met the arrows arc down upon them.

The battle was bloody and almost entirely irrelevant. Non-player character slaying soulless non-player characters by the dozen. Buffs and debuffs exploded across the field like fireworks, exploding with bright neon numbers denoting the extra damage done.

The real show, however, was to take place to the side. Already a row of stalwart defenders had formed up, equipment mismatched, avatars bursting with power.

Kaine felt a thrill go down his spine as he shifted in his seat. He was rapt, pupils dilated, the conversation around him falling away into the ether.

"Light the pitch! Night comes for us all!" Kaine hammered into the chat box. His message spread and his clannies did the dirty work for him. R3FL3XXX ran up beside him and started placing all of his incendiaries atop the siege machine's inventory while FROGGLENN did the same, shoulder to shoulder with him. R3FL3XXX was a mage, the texture of his skin a bedazzling cloak of stardust and supernova. FROGGLENN was a primitive, a barbarian, clad only in a loincloth, his avatar an icon of brute masculine force straight out of the pages of a Robert E. Howard novel.

The great boulders were cut loose and flew through the painted midnight sky as fast as the video card could render it. Kaine never noticed, never made the distinction. To him, it was nighttime. Even though the boys hadn't hustled down the the meal hall just yet for a midnight snack, for Kaine, the raid -- and his part to play -- was everything.

His own army stretched out behind him, twenty strong and bolstered with hundreds of husks holding mortal weapons. Commons, bolstered only by the passive bonuses that Kaine and his allies had gathered in preparation for the raid. Good food, properly brewed potions, the footsoldiers of the invading force were juiced to the gills.

"Charge!!!" Kaine ordered, hammering the keys. He had a headset on, but voicechat would slow the DSL connection to the server too much to effectively command. It was up to his guildmates to chat if they so chose, but most knew the procedure and proper responses as if it were second nature.

Then everything when black, and his universe imploded.

"What the hell?!" Kaine said, yanking the headset from his ears.

His new roommate, whose name Kaine couldn't recall, pointed down between his legs with an ogrish grin.

The floor was an inch deep with beer, his own jeans soaked black from the splashing of legs in tune with the acoustic jam. Island tunes ripped from the throats of a dozen drunk students in various sorts of inebriation, some with arms wrapped about their neighbour's necks.

Kaine got down on all fours, ignoring the party. His power bar had gone dark, the rich amber LED gone out. Hopefully the surge had protected the power supply and motherboard from damage. He didn't need his subwoofer and speakers in any case, and he yanked his monitor, tower, and speakers free by the plugs, setting the two former in place much higher up, directly into the outlet carved into the concrete wall.

He got back into his chair and hit the power button, breathing a sigh of relief as the blue brights around his case fans shot to life. The BIOS screen rolled over his monitor and everything checked out fine. His anger abated, he turned to survey the racket.

His old roommate, Curtis, and his new roommate who he still couldn't put a name on, were swinging bottles of the local bitter and pushing each other around playfully, cheeks full blush. Next to them, legs swinging down from the simple cot placed lengthwise hard against the wall, the twins. Two girls who had the reputation of spending the night with one lucky person at any given rager. Though they shared the same dusky complexion, wide hips, and long black hair, they were not related, and seemed to be in an on-again, off-again relationship that tempestuous at best. Matching wine glasses were clasped in their long-fingered grip, white knuckled so as not to spill a spot of pinot grigio.

They were sitting on the lap of the biggest boy on campus, Bronlo. Bronlo was an exchange student from overseas. Big, strong, and with a larger than life smile and personality, there was hardly a kid from the house that didn't like Bronlo. Looks like he'd drawn the straight flush tonight, Kaine noted to himself.

He wasn't sure how he kept getting drawn into these encounters. On his application card for on-campus residence, he'd listed all of his personal preferences honestly. Interests: Computer games, jazz, fantasy and science fiction, fishing, four-wheeling, geocaching. Aversions: Jocks, Snobs, and nosey folks.

Somehow, he'd ended up with the best and worst of both worlds.

"You bastards wrecked my power bar!" Kaine tossed out to a peal of laughter in reply. Several swaying hands proferred a beverage in a dark brown bottle. He snagged one and slugged it down. What was lost was lost. He wouldn't be able to log in for at least ten minutes anyway.

As the song stay the same, and he waited for his CPU to process and execute everything it needed to in order to prepare to launch, he sipped his Baron and thought about the future.

Would he win the battle?

Would he win the war?

The alcohol gave him a surety that he rarely felt, it's bitter body wrapping itself about his bones.

CHAPTER 09
ANTI / HERO

Kaine was too old to cry anymore. His eyes were dry and the loose flesh that surrounded them showed all the signs of surrender to the years. His leg was swollen and very sore from the long walk home, having taken the better part of the day. The sun had beat down on his back mercilessly, the dry heat sapping his strength and what remained of his resolve. The empty stretch of road that led away from the factory back into the city was featureless, offering scant in the way of scenery but a few gnarled shrubs and the odd roadkill in various states of decay.

He survived the marathon, though, and as the dulcet orange of sunset brought with it the cool promise of a sweet summer's night, Kaine crested the city outskirts. Greeting him was a tourist trap, a strip of mini-businesses and street vendors, accompanied by the buzzing rotors of drones darting overhead. The scent of roasted meat caused him to salivate, spending whatever water reserves he had left. Succumbing to his dire thirst, he ambled up to a gaudy streetcart and hailed the vendor, fishing through his pants pocket for loose change. Coming up with nearly ten dollars, he bought two ice cold Barons and left two quarters as a tip. Public drunkenness was no longer a charge, nor nuisance, as it was lucrative business to ship habitual violators off to a private prison somewhere in the national aether.

Leaning against the cart, ignoring the admonishments of the meatslinger, Kaine took in the scene around him for a few moments. On the outskirts, the safest part of the city, every night was like Mardi Gras in New Orleans. Or at least the popular imaginings of it.

Ropelights in every colour of the rainbow were strung from the balconies of low-slung hostels and motels, many tackily-dressed tourists crowding their balconies with beverages in hand, observing and pointing at items of interest.

The small drones, like bumblebees drunk on nectar, buzzed about lazily, their cameras scrutinizing all of the buying and selling and dancing and cursing with a detached yet unwavering dedication. On their underbellies, nestled up against the manufacturer's logo, rested more than a few advertisements pushing artisan wares and local handicrafts. Whether or not it drove conversion was irrelevant, it was all about raising awareness and perpetuating the symbol and the name in the minds of so many, consciously or unconsciously. Meta-marketing, Kaine thought he'd heard it called on the streams. Really, just repackaged sales techniques from an earlier era with a new coat of paint.

Noisy, dirty electronic music boomed from the Factory, a nearby dancehall. Lasers shot out from the roof and cascaded down over the crowd at regular intervals, pulsing in tune with the pumping bass. Hammered teen-agers and scantily clad ladies screeched at one another, shrieking with delight, bacchanalian dreaming. Some ravers, hair dyed shocking shades of green, purple, pink, and blue, streamed from the alley-door of the Factory and dissolved into the general madness of the crowd, searching for more alcohol to continue the party or for street sausages and sports drink to take the edge off.

Kaine simply leaned and drank double fisted.

"Hell of a night."

The comment came from beside him. Kaine was too tired to do anything else but look over. He saw a tall man wearing a neat pinstriped suit, along with a sharp trilby. Not something you saw every day.

"Yeah. Sure is. Hell of a day, too," Kaine said from behind his shades.

"Wear those at night? Old enough to appreciate a Corey Hart joke?" the stranger inquired, corners of his mouth tugging upward.

"Heard that one before. Got anything original?" Kaine replied.

"As a matter of fact, detective, I do. I was just hoping we could have a little levity before the real fun began. I've had work done on my eyes, too. It's really nothing to be ashamed of."

The set of the stranger's smile crumbled, and now he looked grimly serious. Kaine now noticed the peculiar meltwater blue of the businessman's irises.

"Well, I've about had it up to here," Kaine lifted his bottle of Baron and drew the wet mouth of the glass across the underside of his chin, "with surprises today. Spit it out or get lost son. And I ain't a goddamn detective anymore. Wish I didn't have to keep telling people that."

The well-dressed man appraised Kaine, and the ex-cop read him in return.

"You're not the least bit curious as to how I know your name and former occupation?"

"Information is the cheapest thing you can buy in today's world. I'm a nobody, an ant. You could buy my record for a fraction of what that fine suit you're wearing would cost. So no, I'm not curious as to how you mined that data. What I am curious about is why you would want that info. It's worthless. Smart people don't pay for bum tips."

"And if you were a bum, as you so dearly profess, you would be right. But that's not the whole story, is it?"

The stranger smoothed out the wrinkles in his suit and straightened his floral necktie. The crisp white linen of his collared shirt beneath gave Kaine the impression that this was a man of means.

Kaine didn't reply, waiting for the mysterious man to make his pitch.

"Let's take a walk, shall we? I have something to show you."

Kaine raised an eyebrow in response, not moving from his spot, still leaning against the cart. The fat fellow selling street meat and beers behind the dirty countertop appeared to have heard nothing, his attention pointedly elsewhere. He would punctuate their odd conversation with cupped hands to his moustached mouth, hawking his best price to passersby.

"Look, if I intended violence, I would have picked you

off during your long walk home. Trust me, if only for a short while."

Kaine pushed off of the cart, leaving an empty with the vendor who nodded his small appreciation. He hammered back another long pull as he limped up to stand akimbo to the stranger. They left the party at their backs, strolling down a long boulevard that cut to the city center.

"Where are we going?"

"That's a secret, sir. If I told you, I'd have to kill you."

Seeing Kaine's eyes widen, the stranger laughed. "Another old joke. I'm sure you get the reference."

Kaine cursed under his breath, not finding it particularly funny. The pair went on in silence. The lights in the office buildings and banks towering above slowly clicked off, one by one, leaving an abstract array of perfect rectangles shining against black obelisks. It was incidental art, architectural and artificial.

"Beautiful, aren't they? Each time it's a different scene. Transient in nature. Some people stay late to work, often-times overnight. Not me, of course. That's one of the perks of being a boss," the stranger bragged, pride carrying through his tone.

"Most of the work is automated now. Those things are relics. Why do they still stand? There's no need for them anymore, or even the people that work there. Bots take care of everything else, and they do the real banking and business, too. Explain that to me." Kaine took him up on his braggadocio, both men drawing to a halt at the end of a narrow alleyway. On one side, a shuttered second-hand clothier. On the other side was a run-down laundromat, sparsely attended given the late hour.

"Well, Mr. Kaine, the reason is simple..."

The stranger grunted slightly while pushing past him, turning shoulder first to navigate the alley while taking great care not to scrape the sides with his expensive threads. Kaine followed suit, though he protected his remaining Baron rather than his old work uniform.

"... it's a statement. It's an impressive visual reminder. It's strength. It's power. It's influence. It's dominant and pervasive. When you look up, you see us. No matter where you are in the city, you see my skyscraper and you know what it represents. You don't know the people who work there. They change, they fade away, they retire and are fired. The building, though. It's forever. Like our business. We want you to remember that. Well, not you personally. We have other plans for you."

The stranger's face was obscured to him, and so Kaine couldn't discern the intent of his ambiguous reply, even if he understood the philosophy behind the answer. Beneath their feet lied a morass of mixed rubbish: black roaches, plastic liquor bags, and torn posters advertising the memory of punk rock.

"Ah, we're here."

Kaine caught up to his travelling companion. They stood in front of a plain looking door, red to match the masonry. Paint was peeling in great tears down the face of the door, revealing weathered wood beneath. A brushed aluminum panel was screwed into the door at about waist height on the right hand side. The stranger raised his wrist to the panel and the sound of a heavy bolt being withdrawn could be heard, dulled by the concrete and the wood enveloping it.

The door swung open. A shaft of pure, radiant white washed over the pair. Kaine squinted despite the shades, raising a forearm to cover his eyes. The stranger walked inside without missing a beat. Turning, and extending his hand to Kaine, he appeared almost god-like.

"Need a hand?" he asked of his elder.

Kaine pushed the stranger's hand aside with the neck of his bottle and awkwardly lurched inside, still favouring his good leg. The pain remained.

It was an enormous chamber. The walls, ceiling, and floor were the shade of fresh snow. There were glass desks manned by extremely attractive men and women, all clad in purest white. It was like walking into a vision of the future from Kaine's childhood, not the filthy reality that had come to pass. He had no words. Even his beer, hanging from slack fingers, was forgotten.

They walked the wide aisle that seperated the neat rows of desks, each attendant taking the time to pause from their work on the transparent terminals to greet the businessman as they passed.

"Hello, Mr. Ames."

"Good evening, Mr. Ames!"

"How nice of you to bring a visitor, Mr. Ames."

The warm welcome continued all the way down the line, porcelain white teeth and stunning smiles on every face. Whether it was genuine was beyond even Kaine's ability to deduce, so perfect was the scenery. He now noticed, at the periphery of the room, a number of androids, prototype models he'd never seen before, working away at wall terminals, their movements as fluid and precise as those of a master artist. Flawlessly efficient, he saw them inputting and manipulating solid streams of data as if it were easy, almost effortless. Perhaps, to them, it was. Their long limbs and slender bodies gave them a graceful aesthetic that was absent from the bulky factory-made models common to the life he had known before this place.

"A world within a world," Kaine whispered. Ames must have heard him, for he crooked his neck as they walked to peer at the old man's weathered face. Seeing surprise and child-like wonder written there, Ames capitalized on the opportunity to deepen the conversation.

"Yes, Mr. Kaine. I'm sure this is all a bit overwhelming on such short notice. As with all things, the propensity for human beings to make magical truths into mundane matters. I see this every day of my life, and have been privileged since birth to be on the cusp of cutting edge tech. It is always nice to be reminded and humbled by this. Please, if you need a moment..."

He looked expectantly at Kaine. The dozens of beautiful people pretended not to notice, but their disinterest was transparent. They, too, expected an answer from the unexpected guest.

"No. I'll be fine. It's just ... I never ... this is something out of a science fiction novel. Truly. Hidden dens of high technology. Businessmen who aren't all that they seem. Secret societies. Is this reality?"

Ames chuckled graciously, and his servants joined in chorus. It made Kaine more nervous, not less.

"No, no, no, please Mr. Kaine. I can assure you that this is certainly real life. I can also assure you that this is in no way a secret society -- after all, BioPlay is a publicly traded company. Something which you are most certainly aware. And though we don't advertise this particular facility, you can rest assured that it is entirely legal."

Ames sought a reassuring narrative. It escaped Kaine, who was growing increasingly uncomfortable. The suicide booths were entirely legal, and they were a double-edged blade that permeated his life with a certain lethality. Like the mythical Sword of Damocles, perpetually suspended above his balding head, Kaine felt like he was likewise caught in a complex trap, even -- or especially -- here. BioPlay was the company that ran the booths, a third of the banks on the continent, and who knows what other splintered subsidiaries in every market that a middleman could meddle in. BioPlay was everywhere -- more powerful than any government, more insidious than any disease, more benevolent on the surface than any church.

They reached the end of the line. Everyone had returned to their work as if nothing had happened. There was a single door in front of them, bearing the same brushed metal panel as the misleading wooden door in the alleyway. Again, Ames brought his wrist to bear against the cold steel and the door gave way with a hiss.

"After you." Ames stood clear of the frame and let Kaine limp through first.

The room was as spotless as the rest of the facility. All of the decor was post-modern, a return to cubes and squares and triangles and everything else with perfectly measured angles. A study looking bookshelf was home to an array of paper books, their spines the only hint of colour in the otherwise sterile setting. They were also exceedingly rare, leatherbound volumes that spoke to being at least a century old, if not more. Most paper and ink volumes had been shredded and recycled into presswood or prefab shelters a long time ago.

"Who has the time to read anymore, Mr. Kaine? I see you admiring my collection. I can assure you that those tomes are exceedingly expensive. Yet of the market that exists for them, barely any of the collectors bother to read the actual texts. It's all for show, you see. Scarcity. Like the world about us. Nobody has the means to afford what they have, so they borrow. They borrow from people like me and my associates. Then we make them pay us back. Been that way since the earliest days of mercantilism, then capitalism, now corporatism. Natural order of things, sad to say."

Kaine let Ames philosophize to his heart's content. It gave him time to collect his thoughts and to collect more clues as to what his place was in the grand scheme the magnate was concocting. He had never been much of a book reader in any case, never romanticizing the printed page. Both men assessed each other, Kaine in his comfortable white pleather chair and Ames seated behind his one of a kind desk, custom-crafted by an artist whose name he couldn't remember.

"Get to the deal, Ames. I'm a nameless, never-was nobody with a bad leg and a broken family. I'm going to turn seventy in a handspan of years. My best days are behind me. Most of my friends are dead, from the bottle or the booth or the simple truth of scarcity. Starvation. Addiction. Poverty. Hopelessness. These are the demons of our time. My wife is a wasted mess. My kids, I barely see them, and I know they're out there somewhere with a rail up their nose and a needle in their arm, wasting away the same way."

This seemed to amuse the man in the flashy suit. Ames laughed softly to himself, leaning back in his luxuriously padded chair. He adjusted his necktie, tightening it. A secretary with long, slender legs knocked at the door. Ames waved her off as one would an irritating insect, never taking his eyes from Kaine's face.

"Well, Mr. Kaine. Much of that may be true. You would know better than I. I don't live with the people; I live above them. I wouldn't go so far as to call myself a puppeteer, but I do pull the strings that jar and jangle so many lives of those who dwell below. This is the truth of our shared reality. As above, so below. But, I can't help but take issue with one thing you've said."

"And that is?" Kaine asked bitterly.

"You're not a nobody. Nor a never-was. And we can pay for your leg, and more, if you'd like to prove it."

Kaine's eyes narrowed behind his mirrored lenses.

"Ah. Suspicion. The first response of all of my best clients. And that is what you are, whether or not you accept my proposal. Should you reject the idea, of course, you are free to go. I'll continue to monitor you, to watch you for a moment of weakness, and then I'll come to you again. This time with a weaker offer, a withered olive branch if you will. But!"

And for this, Ames spread his arms wide in a magnificent gesture.

". . . but! If you accept my offer now, in full, you will reap the entirety of the benefits I am prepared to bestow upon you. My wealth is great, Mr. Kaine, but my appreciation runs deeper and holds truer."

Kaine brought the Baron to his lips and finished it off, then bent to lay the empty bottle on the floor. The lacing remained, sticking to the inside of the glass, slowly settling. Still, he said nothing.

"Every negotiation starts with an ask, Kaine, and you've asked for nothing. I know you. I've watched you. Well, my operatives have. Two thousand dollars on a top night. Three to five hundred most nights. Never in the bottom 10 except on very rare occasions, and if you hit the bottom five, you stop playing for a few weeks to sober up. Total earnings over the nearly ten years you've been hitting the booths? Nearly a quarter million dollars. Now I know that kind of money isn't much in a world where inflation runs rampant and even the bare necessities of life cost dozens of hard-earned dollars. Where did the rest go? Down your throat, down her throat, or to pay off the loan sharks you use on the regular to cover the rest of the bills. Kids blow it on drugs and joyrides, not their education. The implants you need for your leg are a million, easy. I can give you that. I can give you that and much more."

Kaine was interested. The thought of being able to wake up in the morning without the dull ache that told him he was going to have to face another day on pins and needles was enticing. The thought of having enough money to tell the loan sharks to go fuck themselves was even stronger. The idea of never having to envision his children selling their bodies or their sweat for scraps was irresistible.

"Show me, Ames. Show me what you want from me."

As if on cue, the door opened behind Kaine. The same secretary that had been dismissed earlier had returned, pushing something on smooth castors across the highly polished floor. She rounded them both and delivered her burden to the side of Ames' desk.

Bakunawa stood there, tall and proud. Fully restored, the marquee gleaming with bold confidence, the monitor with nary a smudge, the joystick and buttons in exactly the same position that Kaine remembered them. The matte black siding of the arcade cabinet was powder perfect, without blemish.

The secretary, long brown hair bouncing with every step, face of carved ivory, smoothly knelt and grabbed the thick power cord from the back of the machine, running it to a nearby outlet. The monitor popped, crackled, and then delivered the pixelated attract screen. The speakers rumbled, the distorted cry of the silver dragon echoed about the room. She left without saying a word, her dress, her heels, and the flesh of her lithe back nearly indistinguishable from each other, all a part of her as a figure.

"This is what I want from you, Mr. Kaine. One chance to leave the pit of rats and misfits, fighting to the death over a pittance, a purse worth less than an hour of my time, an audience of hundreds at most."

Kaine's hands started to tremble, fear returning to him in nauseous waves.

"I see I have upset you, Mr. Kaine, and that's not my intention. Or, rather, it may be, should you prove false to your playing record. You see, I offer you a choice. Play, and win, and leave here a million dollars richer and with a professional gaming contract in hand. Each match for a hundred thousand or more if you finish in the money. Play, and lose, and you don't leave here alive. Can't have you spreading secrets about town without having you on the hook, you see. Not if your value is in doubt, in any case."

"So what you said earlier, about leaving, about saying no, was just a lie? You don't intend to let me leave here without being on your leash Ames. We both know that." Kaine rasped, folding his arms in front of him.

"Smart man. I guess you never stopped being a detective after all."

Ricky Kaine sighed. It was the release of so much anger, doubt, and despair.

Then he stood, his joints creaking with the effort. He knocked over the empty.

He limped over to the cabinet. He ran his hand over the wood, over the smooth plastic, over the slits of the coin mech. He felt Ames standing next to him, pressing hot metal into his palm. The ridges told him it was a quarter. They'd been out of circulation for fifteen years.

He heard the door open at his back and the sound of footsteps, many footsteps, one after the other. He could feel the eyes on the nape of his neck, around the slope of his shoulders. He knew they were there to witness.

Again, his nemesis called out to him, screeching in a language that only he understood. He looked into the eyes of the dragon.

I haven't forgotten you, never, not during all these years -- Ricky Kaine spoke to the figment on the screen in his head. And the great wyrm, scales shining against the empty vacuum of space, flying over the poor defenses of the moon, replied.

Play me.

Touch me.

Show them.

Show yourself.

The sound of the quarter rolling down the coin slot.

The hands, veined, fibrous, scarred -- on the buttons.

The high score awaiting his initials.

The audience chanting his name.

The dragon.

Doom.

THE XANDER DREW SERIES

Prologue: The Long Road (May 2014)

Book One: Cinders (April 2015)
Book Two: Sinister Intent (November 2015)
Book Thee: Faith (December 2017)
Book Four: Family Values (forthcoming)

COMING SOON FROM ENGEN BOOKS:

FAMILY VALUES

While hunting the vile crime lord Stephen Fields, Xander discovers a string of kidnappings going back nearly forty years that always result in the child being returned, years later, dead. With the help of his new friend - and mother-to-be - Lisa Rowdan, Xander must discover the sinister origins of a plot that has existed in Los Angeles for generations.

The early years of **Xander Drew** as he struggles with the evils of his small rural hometown of Coral Beach, Maine. Cursed with the heart of the Womb and the gift of seeing the world around him for what it really is, Xander must learn the hard lessons about the nature of humanity to traverse the minefield of criminals, gangs, and abusers that stand between him and ultimate happiness -- but most of all that **sometimes it takes a monster, to catch a monster.**

"THE WRITING OF ITS GENERATION- - VISUAL, TO-THE-POINT AND IN-THE-MOMENT."
- The Northeast Avalon Times

The Coral Beach Casefiles series by Matthew LeDrew:

Book One: Black Womb (October 2007)
Book Two: Transformations in Pain (April 2008)
Book Three: Smoke and Mirrors (February 2009)
Book Four: Roulette (October 2009)
Book Five: Ghosts of the Past (April 2010)
Book Six: Ignorance is Bliss (October 2010)
Book Seven: Becoming (April 2011)
Book Eight: Inner Child (November 2011)
Book Nine: Gang War (April 2012)
Book Ten: Chains (April 2013)

Epilogue: The Long Road (May 2014)

For more information, please visit

www.engenbooks.com

infinity

The world is changing, and we have to change with it. That was the one thing that Victor was really sure of when he started looking for special people: people who could change the possibilities of the future from something certainly grim... to something *infinitely* positive.

Now four unsuspecting people from different backgrounds and walks of life have been thrown into the mix together, and nothing will ever be the same. But there's a difference between hoping for a better world and actually having one, and there will always be resistance to change.

Book One: Infinity (October 2010)
Book Two: The Tourniquet Reprisal (October 2012)
Book Three: Exodus of Angels (April 2016)

Related Books:

Compendium (October 2009)
light|dark (April 2012)
Roulette (October 2009)
The Long Road (May 2014)

Written by the superstar author team of Ellen Curtis (*Compendium*) and Matthew LeDrew (the *Xander Drew* series).

Destiny doesn't wait for anyone.

ABOUT THE AUTHOR

Nicholas Morine (B.A., M. Phil.) grew up reading Harlan Ellison, Stephen King, and John Steinbeck and has never been able to shake the addiction.

His work is provocative, action-oriented, and always incorporates a sense of place and philosophy into the narrative.

From Wolfville, Nova Scotia, Morine has a great affinity for the rural, the popular, and the accessible.

Heavy metal is his religion and the great rock Newfoundland is his second home.